ANNIE'S NEW BEGINNING

Amish Romance

BRENDA MAXFIELD

Tica House Publishing

Sweet Romance that Delights and Enchants!

Personal Word from the Author

Dearest Readers,

Thank you so much for choosing one of my books. I am proud to be a part of the team of writers at Tica House Publishing who work joyfully to bring you stories of hope, faith, courage, and love. Your kind words and loving readership are deeply appreciated.

I would like to personally invite you to sign up for updates and to become part of our **Exclusive Reader Club**—it's completely Free to join! We'd love to welcome you!

Much love,

Brenda Maxfield

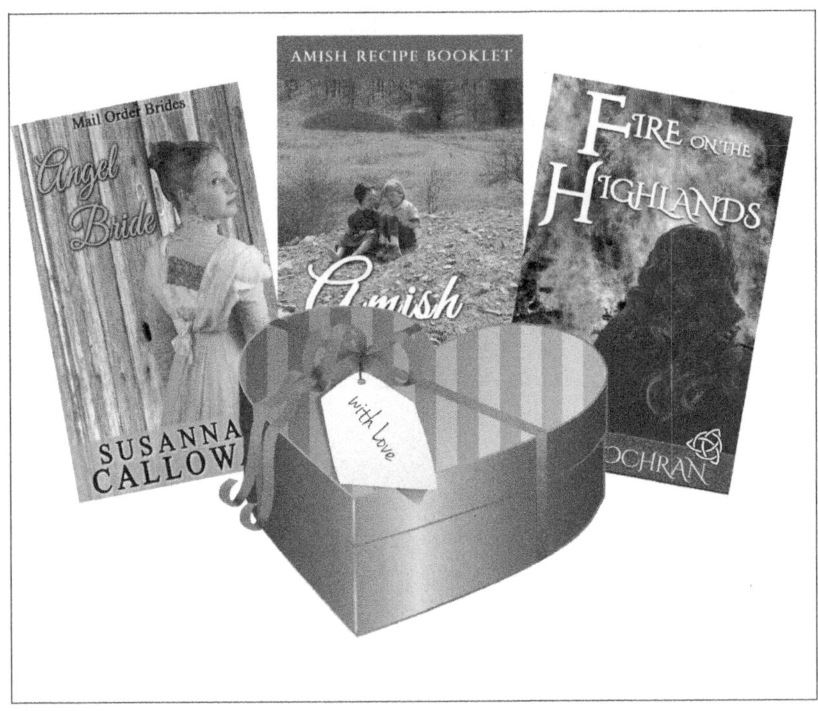

VISIT HERE to Join our Reader's Club and to Receive Tica House Updates:

https://amish.subscribemenow.com/

Chapter One

> Remember ye not the former things, neither consider the things of old...
>
> — ISAIAH 43:18 KJV

Annie Hershberger rushed back into the house and slammed the door. After the frigid air outside, the heat from the warming stove was stifling. She tried to gulp in a breath. She tried to still her racing heart. She tried to keep her tears from falling.

"What's happened?" her mother asked, coming into the room with a frown. "Why am I hearing doors being slammed?"

"I-I didn't mean to slam it," Annie said, forcing herself to hold it together.

Her mother smiled. "What did Matthew want?" Her smile faded as she seemed to actually see her daughter. Her brow lowered. "What's wrong, Annie?"

She stepped forward, but Annie drew back.

"Nothing. Nothing's wrong."

Violet frowned. "Something is clearly wrong."

"*Nee*," Annie said, swallowing hard. She slipped out of her cloak and hug it on its peg. She couldn't bear to tell her mother that her engagement was off—not when only an hour ago, Violet was happily making plans for the wedding. Not when only a few hours ago, Annie had told her mother she was engaged in the first place.

"Annie Hershberger, tell me the truth. For sure and for certain, I can see by your face something's wrong."

"I-I..." Annie bit her lip. Then she shook her head and ran up the stairs to her bedroom. She slammed that door, too, and threw herself on the bed. How could he have done it? How could Matthew have broken off their engagement not twenty-four hours after asking her to marry him?

She squeezed her eyes shut and let the tears come. It hadn't even been a full day...

And then she jolted upright. Her mouth dropped open and she froze. Wait. *Wait.* Her mind played back over the scene in Matthew's buggy the night before.

He never asked me. He never said the words. Bile rose in her throat and she only barely kept herself from vomiting. She remembered everything with excruciating clarity. He'd been going to ask her to marry him. He had—of that she was sure. But he couldn't get the words out. She'd stupidly thought he was only nervous. And quite unlike herself, she'd taken matters into her own hands.

Jah, jah, I'll marry you, she'd said. Her eyes widened. She'd seen Matthew's look then. The complete shock on his face. At the time, she'd skimmed right over it, so thrilled to be engaged. And then, he'd smiled, and she completely forgot his look of surprise and bewilderment. She'd started right in, too, jabbering about the wedding and their plans and how wonderful being married was going to be.

Dearest God in heaven.

What had she *done?* Why, she'd barreled right on through when he hadn't even asked her. And now she knew—with complete humiliation—that he wouldn't have asked her. He wouldn't have gotten the words out.

Dear, dear, dear Gott. What have I done?

She fell back on her bed again and stared unblinkingly at the ceiling. Being December, the days were short, and dusk was already falling outside the window. Shadows of naked, flickering branches stretched across her ceiling. She looked at them, unseeing. All she could see in her mind's eye was the total fool she'd made of herself the night before.

Matthew must have been in agony, listening to her blather on and on about their wedding. He must have wanted to escape in the worst way. Why hadn't he said anything? Why hadn't he set her straight?

Ach, but it must have been a nightmare for him.

Matthew. Matthew. Matthew. Why didn't you stop me?

Because Matthew was kind. And loving. And gentle. All the reasons she'd fallen in love with him in the first place. He didn't stop her because of who he was. He hadn't wanted to hurt her.

But, oh, he *had* hurt her. On the porch. Just now. She closed her eyes and the tears seeped from her closed lids. It was over. Matthew was gone. The man she loved didn't love her back. Didn't want to marry her. Had it *all* been fake? Had he never cared for her even a little?

Why had he done it? Why had he courted her?

But she knew why, and the knowledge sliced through her heart. Matthew had tried to distract himself from the girl he really loved. She, Annie, was his distraction. She was his effort to steer himself away from his true love.

Annie sucked in a breath and pressed her hand against her chest.

Matthew loved his cousin, Doris. No, he didn't just love Doris, he was *in love* with her. Annie had always known he had a special relationship with Doris. The two of them had been close for as long as she'd known him. But she'd never guessed—never even dared to imagine—that it was more than that. She'd completely forgotten—or ignored—the fact that Matthew and Doris weren't truly related. That they weren't truly cousins. He had been raised by Doris's aunt and uncle, but he wasn't blood kin.

Why hadn't she realized? Hadn't she noticed how Matthew's eyes lit up whenever he talked about Doris? Hadn't she noticed how he always volunteered to drive her wherever she needed to go? Hadn't she noticed his upset when Doris had another beau?

Ach, but she'd been blind. Blind and *stupid.*

She turned on her side, and her tears dripped down onto her quilt. It was cold up here in her room. The heat from the warming stove downstairs helped very little upstairs. She didn't like the cold, but she made no move to cover herself. There was a knock on her door and her mother came in, holding a lantern which she set down on Annie's bedside table.

"I've given you a minute," she said, "but now I want to know. What's happened between you and Matthew? Did you have a quarrel? These things happen sometimes, daughter. It happens with all couples. You and Matthew will make up and all will be well."

"*Nee, Mamm*," Annie managed to eke out. "All will not be well."

Violet moved to the bed and sat down beside Annie, rubbing her shoulder. "You'll see," she said softly. "It will all work itself out."

Annie shook her head. "It won't," she cried. "It's over."

Violet's hand on her shoulder stopped moving. "What? What do you mean?"

"I'm... We're not engaged anymore."

Violet stood and faced her. "What? What do you mean?"

Annie gulped in a breath. "Just what I said, *Mamm*. It's over."

"How can it be over when it's only just begun?" Violet's voice rose with each word. "You're making no sense, daughter."

Annie struggled to sit up. She swiped the tears from her eyes. "I'm not engaged. Matthew doesn't love me."

The light from the lantern flickered over her mother's incredulous expression. "How can that be? He asked you to marry him!"

"That's another thing," Annie said, her voice leaden. "It seems I... Well, he never asked me."

"What?" Violet's eyes stretched wide. "What are you *talking about?*"

"I jumped the gun, *Mamm*. He was going to ask me, but he didn't actually say the words—"

"*What?*" Violet cried again.

Annie sighed. "He was going to ask, but the words were never spoken." She drew in a shaky breath. "But I... I... I told him I'd marry him."

"Without him *even asking?*" Violet's voice climbed to an incredible pitch. "How could you, Annie? How could you be *so forward?*"

Anger rushed through Annie—her ears rang with it. And she had no idea who she was angry at. Matthew? Her mother? Herself?

Or all of them.

"It's not like I did it on purpose!" she snapped back. "He was *going* to ask me. He was. How was I to know he'd change his mind?"

Her bitter tone whipped through the air. She tensed and then the breath seeped out of her. Her shoulders dropped and she slumped, feeling completely dejected.

"But Annie, he didn't set you straight? He let you go on and on?"

"He let me go on and on," Annie whispered, her heart breaking all over again.

"*But why?* Why was he courting you?"

"I was convenient."

"*Convenient?* What are you talking about?"

"He's in love with Doris—"

"Doris? His *cousin,* Doris?" Violet gasped.

"They're not related."

Confusion rippled across Violet's features, and then she sucked in a breath. "*Nee*. You're right. They're not. Oh, dear Lord."

Violet sank down on the bed beside Annie again. Annie leaned against her shoulder.

"I'm so sorry, daughter. Truly sorry. So, that was why he came by? To break it off."

"That was why he came by."

Violet bit her lip and then slipped her arm around Annie's shoulder. "It must be for the best," she mumbled. "Matthew wasn't the one for you. Someone better will come along. You'll see."

Annie closed her eyes and tears slipped from beneath her lids. She didn't want someone else to come along. She wanted Matthew. *Matthew!*

Violet stood back up. "I'll go make you a nice steamy cup of hot chocolate," she said. "That'll make you feel better. Come on down in a few minutes." She bent and kissed the top of Annie's *kapp*, then she picked up the lantern and left the room.

Hot chocolate? Did her mother think she could fix this with *hot chocolate?*

The total absurdity of it made Annie want to scream. But she didn't. Her mother was trying to help.

But Annie didn't go downstairs in a few minutes. She pulled back her quilts and got into bed, clothes and all, and she didn't stir until morning.

Chapter Two

Christmas Day was miserable. All Annie could think about was that she was supposed to be excited about her engagement. She was supposed to be savoring the knowledge all day, rejoicing in her future. It was supposed to be the best Christmas Day of her entire life. Instead, she buried herself in the kitchen, serving the meal, ensuring everyone had enough to eat, making certain the desserts were replenished the minute the dishes were emptied. She even refused help when *redding* up the kitchen.

"You don't have to do this yourself," her mother admonished. "We have plenty of women in this family..."

"*Mamm*, if I have to sit out there and pretend everything is all right, I'll go crazy," Annie told her. "Please, just let me do it—"

"What's going on in here?" her aunt Rose said, entering the kitchen. "Annie, we've hardly seen you all day. Get on out here and let your *mamm* and me finish up."

Annie forced herself to smile. "*Nee.* Consider this my Christmas gift to you, *Aenti.* You and *Mamm* go on back out there and visit."

"But your cousins are wondering where you are." Rose laughed. "And they aren't thinking a bit about *redding* up the kitchen. They're wanting to move on to opening the few gifts."

"I'll be right out," Annie assured her. She raised her hands and made a show of scooting the two older women out of the kitchen. Rose laughed again and acquiesced. So did Violet; although, she threw Annie a worried look before disappearing back into the dining area.

When Annie had the kitchen back to herself, she slumped against the counter. *Keep going,* she told herself. *Don't stop now or you'll cry.*

But she wasn't going to cry. She was sick of crying. She didn't want to mope about Matthew anymore. He wasn't worth it. What he'd done was cruel and heartless, and she shouldn't even be giving him a moment of thought.

But he is *worth it,* her heart protested. Matthew was the most wonderful man she'd ever known. She still wanted to be his wife.

Nee. Nee. Nee. Enough.

She plunged her hands into the hot dish water and started scrubbing. *Work.* That helped everything. Staying busy with chores, not letting yourself have a minute to think—that helped. But as she continued to scrub, her mind wouldn't stop, and more than one tear fell into the dishwater.

"Annie!" called her father. "Come on out here. We're going to sing a few songs."

It was the same every Christmas. Her father loved to sing, and he loved the old hymns. He often led the family in a verse or two when they were together. Annie didn't know of one other family that did this. When she was young, she'd thought all families sang together when they gathered, but she'd found out soon enough that she was wrong.

"Hurry up," he called.

She knew there was nothing for it but to comply. Josiah Hershberger would not start the singing until every family member was present. She rinsed off her hands and dried them on the dishtowel her mother had embroidered for Christmas. Then she took a deep breath and went into the front room, where everyone was now gathered.

"*Onkel*, can we sing Christmas carols?" Jill asked, her huge six-year-old eyes wide. "I love them the best."

"I don't see why not," Josiah said with a chuckle. "Let's start with 'Oh, Little Town of Bethlehem.'"

He led with his rich baritone voice and everyone joined in. Annie squished herself onto the davenport beside her cousin Jeb. He gave her a playful jab in the ribs, and despite everything, she laughed. As the singing got underway, Annie was able to put aside her grief—at least, for a short while. It felt good to concentrate on something else. The voices around her were strong and melodious, and they were used to signing together, so they blended beautifully.

"How about 'Silent Night'?" Uncle Charles asked.

"That's a *gut* one," another of Annie's uncles said.

Her father started singing 'Silent Night' in German. It was Annie's favorite song, and always brought a few tears as she imagined that day in the stable, centuries before. When they sang the line, "All is calm, all is bright," her mother gave her a meaningful look. Annie averted her eyes, not wanting to burst into tears in front of everyone.

When the song was over, her aunt Nancy sighed. "Lovely," she said softly. "Just lovely."

Everyone was silent for a moment, even the younger children. It was almost as if a spell had been cast. Then Uncle Peter cleared his throat. "I heard from Hollybrook the other day."

"From Thelma?" Violet asked. "You didn't pass on the letter."

"Not yet," Nancy said. "But Thelma says she needs more help in their toy store. Of course, with Christmas and all, they were right busy, but she says business has picked up in general. So, that's a big blessing for them."

"Needing to hire on someone else? *Jah,* that's *gut* news," Josiah agreed. "I wonder who they'll take on?"

"I'll go," Annie blurted.

Everyone turned to gape at her.

"I mean, well, I could help them," she said, squaring her shoulders. This was just what she needed—an excuse to leave. How fortunate to have one pop up right then. It would be a way for her to never have to face Matthew again. Well—not never, but at least for the foreseeable future.

"B-but..." muttered her mother, and Annie could she was trying to come up with a reason for her not to go.

"That's a wonderful *gut* idea," Josiah said. The look he gave her was so full of understanding that she blanched. Did he know? Had her mother told him that Matthew had dumped her? Annie hadn't thought so, but from the look in his eye, she must be wrong.

"I wanna go help, too," Jill declared. "Can I go, *Mamm?*"

"*Nee*, you can't go, daughter," Nancy said. "You ain't old enough."

"I could help," Jill insisted. "I'm a big help. You told me so."

Nancy laughed. "That I did. But this is for grown-ups only."

Jill scowled. "I'm growing up," she muttered.

Annie was still looking at her father. He smiled at her and nodded, and she let out her breath. If her father approved, she would be going.

"I s'pose you could help," Violet said, but there was still a frown on her face. "But maybe Thelma and Henry have already gotten someone."

"I doubt it," Peter said. "The letter ain't old at all. And what with Christmas..."

"I bet they'll be right glad to have you, Annie," Nancy said, smiling.

Annie put on her best smile. Would Matthew even notice she was gone? She drew in a shaky breath. Of course, he wouldn't. What was she thinking?

"I don't want you to go," Annie's younger sister Betty said. "Who will help me with my school projects?"

"She won't be gone forever," Violet interjected, giving her husband a look.

Josiah shrugged. "We can talk about all this later," he said. "Let's sing another carol, shall we?"

Everyone agreed. While they sang 'We Three Kings', Annie's mind whirled. Maybe she could leave this week, before the new year. This could be her new beginning, for sure and for certain. She could forget all about Matthew Wanner and

Doris Glick. She could forget all about her broken heart and broken dreams.

She could start all over.

Bearing gifts, we travel afar... The words of the song rang through her. She wasn't bearing gifts, and she wasn't really traveling that far, but she was leaving. Leaving Linder Creek.

Leaving Matthew Wanner.

Chapter Three

"You're sure you have everything?" Violet asked her for the hundredth time.

"I'm sure, *Mamm.*" Annie sighed. "I'm staying in *Aenti* Thelma's *daadi haus.* If I need anything, all I have to do is go to the main house and ask."

"I know. I know." Violet gently gripped both Annie's shoulders. She looked deeply into her eyes. "Are you all right, daughter?"

"I'm all right."

"*Gott* is all-knowing. He has a plan for you," she said.

"I know, *Mamm.*" Annie did know. She didn't always *feel* that knowledge, but she had to believe it.

"Matthew wasn't for you," Violet said, and Annie flinched at Matthew's name.

Yes, she believed God had a plan for her, but her pain was still raw. And much to her shame, she found herself resenting Doris Glick throughout the day. She tried not to—how she tried. But Doris's laughing face was etched into her brain. Laughing and joyful and her eyes full of love for Matthew.

Annie's Matthew.

No. *Doris's* Matthew.

"You sure you're fine?" Violet asked again.

Annie blinked hard. "*Mamm*, I'm fine. I'm looking forward to helping *Aenti* and *Onkel*. I'm looking forward to staying for a while in Hollybrook. I've always liked Hollybrook—you know that."

Violet nodded. "*Jah*. I know. You're right. Everything is going to be fine."

It was the first time anyone in their immediate family had ever left Linder Creek, and even though Hollybrook wasn't that far away, it was clear Violet didn't much like the idea.

"I can help with the *kinner*," Annie said. "Thelma will be grateful."

Violet nodded. "I imagine you're right at that."

"I'll write."

"Promise me?"

Annie laughed. "Of course, I promise. *Mamm*, I have to go."

"I know." Violet dropped her hands from Annie's shoulders. "And you can come home anytime you like."

Josiah opened the front door and a rush of cold air came in. "You coming, Annie?"

Annie picked up her suitcase. "I'm coming."

"*Kinner,*" Violet called. "Come tell your sister *gut*-bye!"

Annie's two younger brothers came bounding down the stairs. "Bye," they both said at once.

"Where's Betty?" Annie asked, looking beyond them up the steps.

"She says she's not comin' down," Zeke told her. "She's mad about you goin."

"Betty!" Violet called. "Come down here!"

"We have to go," Josiah said. "Annie will miss her bus."

"I'll write Betty, *Mamm*. Don't worry." Annie gave her a quick hug and then hugged her younger brothers. She'd told her older brother Mark and his family good-bye the day before. She hurried out the door.

"I'll take your bag," Josiah said, taking it from her and putting it in the backseat of the buggy. "Get on in."

Annie looked back at the house, and she caught a movement in one of the upstairs windows. It was Betty, standing there with the curtain pulled to the side. She stared down at Annie, and Annie could see she'd been crying. Annie smiled up at her and waved. Betty's lip protruded even further, but she did manage a wave.

Annie mouthed, "I love you," and waved again. Now, her own eyes were filling with tears. She climbed into the buggy and stared straight ahead.

Josiah snapped the reins, and the buggy jolted into movement. Her bus was in forty-five minutes. They would make it just in time.

Annie hadn't had much occasion to ride a bus in her life. Only once before, as a matter of fact. But she was glad for this trip of a couple hours. It would give her time to compose herself—give her time to pray. It was going to be fine in Hollybrook. In fact, it had been the best decision to make. Thankfully, Annie hadn't seen Matthew since the day he visited and broke her heart. If she ever did see him in the future—and she didn't know how she could avoid it—she'd be much better prepared. She'd be in a completely different place. Who knew? Maybe, she would meet someone in Hollybrook.

She tensed. That wasn't why she was going. In truth, the very idea was unappealing at the moment. But, maybe with time...

She shook her head and closed her eyes.

Something pushed at her elbow, and she opened her eyes to see that the older woman who had been sitting across the aisle, had moved to join her.

"You don't mind, do ya, honey?"

"I-I... *Nee*. I don't mind," Annie said.

"I see you're one of them Amish people," the woman said. She pushed her glasses up the bridge of her nose with her thumb. "I don't mean no offense or nothing, but don't you feel stared at all the time?"

Annie's eyes widened. Did the woman realize how she was staring at her right then? But Annie didn't take offense. She used to get offended when she was gawked and pointed at. But she knew folks were mostly just curious. In truth, she was often curious about the *Englisch*, too, so she supposed that made them even.

"*Jah*, I do feel stared at," she replied.

The woman's gaze softened and then she burst out laughing. "Like I'm starin' at you right now," she said. "Lawd, have mercy. I'm one to talk, ain't I?"

Annie couldn't help but smile. She immediately liked this woman.

"My name is Gertie." The woman shook her head and plumped up her flat gray curls. "Ain't it the most awful name in all the world? Gertie? Sounds like I'm a heifer, don't you think?"

Annie giggled.

"Go ahead," Gertie went on. "Won't hurt my feelings, none. Gertie, the Heifer." She cackled. "But folks take to me well enough."

Annie believed that instantly. "I don't think you're a heifer." As soon as she heard how her words sounded, she clapped a hand over her mouth.

Gertie slapped her playfully on the arm. "See? We're already friends."

Annie lowered her hand and smiled. "That didn't sound *gut*. I'm sorry."

"Don't you fuss about it." Gertie's brow crinkled as she studied Annie's face. "You're a pretty one, ain't you? How come you talk with an accent? Weren't you born here in the good ole US of A?"

"I was born here. We speak Pennsylvania Dutch in our homes, so I s'pose that gives us an accent."

"I see. Pennsylvania Dutch, huh? Why don't you say something to me right now in your language?"

"Kaanscht du muukka funge?"

"Hmm. What does that mean?"

Annie laughed. "Can you catch flies?"

Gertie clapped her hands and laughed. "You got a sense of humor, honey. I asked for that."

Annie smiled and settled back in her seat. She gazed out the window, marveling like always at how the scenery sped by. They passed by things so quickly it was as if they had never existed in the first place.

"You going to Hollybrook?" Gertie asked.

Annie turned to her again. "*Jah.*"

"Me, too. Maybe we'll see each other now and again. Wouldn't that be a kick in the pants?"

"*Jah.* A kick in the pants," Annie said, amused and turning the phrase over in her mind. She liked it and would use it with Betty the next time she saw her.

"I'm going to help out with my granddaughter. She's gone and got herself pregnant. Poor thing is only sixteen years old. My daughter is livid, let me tell you. But, land's sake. It ain't the end of the world, now, is it? I imagine Amber will survive just fine—if my daughter doesn't kill her first." She chuckled, but there was a sad note in it. "Anyway, I'm going to try to keep the peace in the household. Give Amber some support, don't you know."

She pursed her lips and stared at Annie. "I reckon your people don't have these kinds of problems."

Annie flushed. "Not usually. Sometimes, though."

Gertie's brow rose. "Well, you don't say. I never figured that."

Annie shrugged. It was the way of things with the *Englisch*. For some reason, they thought Amish weren't regular people —that they didn't struggle with some of the same temptations that other folks did.

Gertie changed the subject and went on and on about how her neighbor kept goats illegally in her back yard. She laughed as she explained the animals' antic and mischief, thoroughly enjoying her own stories until they pulled into Hollybrook. Annie realized with a start that she hadn't thought about Matthew the entire trip—until that moment.

"Thank you, Gertie," she said, as they both began to gather up their belongings.

"What for, honey?"

"A nice trip," Annie said truthfully.

Gertie chuckled. "My daughter won't like my motor mouth so much. I can promise you that. But Amber won't mind. That granddaughter of mine is something special, she is."

"I hope everything goes well."

The bus lumbered to a stop and Gertie stood up. "Me, too, child. Me, too."

Annie followed Gertie off the bus, wondering if she would

ever see her again. Likely not, but in any case, Annie already had a new friend in Hollybrook, and that felt right good.

"Annie!" Thelma called, waving.

Annie quickly walked toward the buggy where Thelma and Henry stood waiting.

"That all your luggage?" Henry asked, ever practical.

"*Nee*. They put my big suitcase in a compartment under the bus."

"I'll go fetch it. What color is it?"

"It's brown with a black handle. My name is on the tag."

Henry walked off to get her bag, and Thelma took hold of her arm. "*Ach*, but we're glad to have you with us."

Annie glanced over her aunt's shoulder, inside the buggy. She saw four pairs of eyes gazing at her.

"The *kinner* are inside. It's right cold out here." Thelma laughed, the corners of her eyes crinkling. "They're excited to see you. Course they don't remember you, having been way too young the last time they saw you. Bobby ain't never seen you at all."

"I'm eager to say hello," Annie said. And she was—she loved children, loved caring for them.

Thelma opened the buggy door. "*Kinner*, this here is your

cousin, Annie. She's the one who'll be staying in the *daadi haus*."

"That's for *Mammi*," Debbie said, raising her chin.

"*Mammi* is gone," Thelma told her. "You know that."

Annie knew that Thelma's mother had passed on the year before. And now she knew that Thelma's mother had lived in the *daadi haus*. Debbie was clearly affronted that anyone else would be allowed to live there.

"I'll take real *gut* care of the *daadi haus*," she assured Debbie with a smile. "Don't you worry none."

Debbie scowled and made a point of looking away. The other three children simply stared at her with big eyes.

"Scoot on over," Thelma said. "Annie's got to fit in, and her bags, too. Go on. Bobby, you come up here and sit on my lap."

Henry returned with her suitcase, and Annie climbed in back with the children. There was some general moving about until they all got situated. Then Henry climbed in and flicked the reins. The buggy lurched into motion.

"It won't take but about thirty minutes to get home," Thelma told her. "How was your Christmas?"

Miserable, she wanted to answer. Instead, she said, "It was fine. It's always nice when the family can get together."

"Someday, we'll have to go to Linder Creek and join everyone.

But, you know, what with all these *kinner*, it would be a bit stressful."

"We'd love to have you," Annie said, knowing it was true.

"I got a truck," Dale told her, tugging on her sleeve. "My *dat* makes toys, you know."

"I do know that," Annie said. "I can't wait to see your truck. Will you show it to me?"

Dale grinned, a flush of pleasure on his cheeks. "I'll show you the minute we get home."

"She's not living in our house," Debbie told him with great authority. "She's living out back in *Mammi's* house."

"Debbie, that's enough," Henry said. He clicked his tongue at the horse. "Giddy 'up, girl."

"Do you remember much about Hollybrook?" Thelma asked Annie.

"Not a whole lot, but I do remember liking it here."

"*Gut.* We hope you're really happy. We sure do need the help."

Henry turned to look at her. "We'll pay you a salary, so don't you worry none about that. But it won't be too high since we'll be providing you room and board."

Annie smiled. "I'm sure it will be fine." She'd arranged with her father to send most of her salary home to help the family, which was standard for a single Amish girl. However, her father did tell her to keep a small percentage for her own personal use.

They arrived at the house, which Annie remembered well. It was like most Amish houses in Indiana—white, two-storied, with a large wrap-around porch. She saw that Thelma had hung out the laundry, despite the freezing temperatures. It looked to be frozen on the line, the shirts stiff and posed as if someone were wearing them. Annie's mother usually hung clothes in the basement during the winter; although, at times, she used the outside line, especially if she wanted to whiten things up which freezing helped with considerably.

Henry brought the buggy to a stop outside the barn. Everyone clambered out.

"Henry will get you situated in the *daadi haus*," Thelma told Annie. "Then, come on into the big house for supper. Are you hungry?"

"A little."

"And then you can see my truck," Dale said.

"I'd like that."

"C'mon, *kinner*, let's get inside and stoke the fire. Gracious, but it's cold out here."

Henry took out her suitcase and they started across the yard and around back of the house. "I'll see to Sparkle in a moment," he said and laughed. "Debbie named the horse. I think Sparkle is a mighty silly name for a mare, but Debbie insisted."

"I like it," Annie said. They circled the corner of the big house, and Annie saw the *daadi haus* where she would be living. It was compact and tidy-looking. White, like the big house, but only one-story high. It also had an ample covered porch with two rockers sitting side-by-side. When it warmed up, it would be a pleasant place to sit. She had imagined she and Matthew spending many long summer evenings on just such a porch...

Stop, she told herself. *Just stop.*

"Here you go," Henry said, opening the door. The warm air inside was welcome, and Annie saw that there was a fire going in the warming stove.

"Do you remember Marlene Dienner?" Henry asked.

"I do," Annie said. She hadn't thought about Marlene for the longest time, but when she'd last visited Hollybrook, she'd been quite fond of her. "I hope to rekindle our friendship."

"She could use it," Henry said.

"What do you mean?"

"She's been real poorly lately."

"What's wrong?"

Henry shrugged. “Thelma can tell you better than me. But I do feel bad for the girl.”

Annie frowned. She remembered Marlene as energetic and lively and very pretty. What had happened? “I’ll ask Thelma then...”

“I’ll put another log in the stove for you. Look around a bit, make yourself to home, and then come on up to the big house.”

“I will. Thank you, *Onkel*.”

“You’re right welcome,” he said. “We’re the ones thanking you.”

He busied himself with the stove, and Annie wandered off to look around the house. It was a simple set-up, two bedrooms in the back with a bathroom between them. The front of the house where she’d come in was a large room with the kitchen at one end and the front room at the other. There was a small dining table dividing the two areas.

Henry had already stoked up the fire and left. Annie sat down for a minute to get her bearings. She could be happy here. But goodness, it was so quiet, she could hear the fire crackle and pop. She snickered softly. At home, it was never that quiet. There was always somebody around, talking or laughing, or making some kind of noise. This would be different.

Living by herself would be different.

We she up to it? Could she do it? She inhaled deeply and then let her breath seep out slowly between her lips. Of course, she could. Why, there would be time to actually think here. Not that she wanted to think too much. Her thoughts would inevitably go to Matthew, and she most definitely didn't want that. She stood up. It would only take her a few minutes to put away her belongings, mostly clothes. But now, she was curious about Marlene. She'd put her things away later that evening—it wasn't like she had much else to do.

What had happened to her friend? She felt a momentary pang of guilt for not keeping up with her. Why hadn't the two of them written each other? If she remembered correctly, they'd started out writing. One or two, maybe even three letters had been exchanged before it fizzled out. Annie regretted that now.

For now, she'd go inside and ask Thelma about Marlene.

Chapter Four

Levi Swarey picked up the .22 pistol. "I'll get 'em, *Dat*, don't you worry."

Walter scratched his head. "I got to tell you the truth, son. I'm sick of them varmints. They're tearing all the insulation up there. It's a mess."

Levi's younger brother, Caleb, was listening in intently. "I want to shoot 'em."

"You ain't old enough," Walter told him, ruffling Caleb's hair. "Your time will come soon enough."

"Can I sneak up there with you?" he asked Levi.

Levi shook his head. "*Nee.* The less noise, the better. I need to catch them unaware."

"I can be quiet," Caleb insisted. "Can't I, *Dat*? I can be quiet."

"*Jah*, son, you can be quiet. But Levi is in charge of this, and he's going to do it his way."

"Can we make a coon hat? In school, there was a picture of this guy with a hat made out of a raccoon skin. The tail was on it and everything."

"We ain't making no coon hat," Walter said, chuckling.

Levi held up his hand, listening. They were standing in the upstairs hallway, and usually the raccoons made enough noise to know when they were in the attic. "Are they up there now?"

"I don't know. Likely. They sleep a lot during the day."

"I seen one during the day before," Caleb said. "Out behind the barn, near the coop."

"Another reason, I'm sick of them," Walter said. "Stealing eggs is bad enough, but tearing the house apart is something altogether different. And I'm getting right tired of worrying about holes in the roof."

"I'll get them." Levi pulled down the attic stairs and listened again. He didn't much like using the pistol, but sometimes it was necessary. His father had taught him how to shoot when he was twelve years old, a year older than Caleb was right now. They'd set up tin cans for targets on the top of fence posts out back by the fields. Levi got the hang of it right away. At first, he thought it was great fun, but when he witnessed one of his friends shoot a bird, he changed his mind.

Now, he took up the gun only when it was absolutely necessary. And he figured raccoons tearing up the insulation in the attic was one of those necessary times. In truth, one of the critters was continually chewing a hole right through the roof shingles which Levi was getting tired of patching.

He crept up the steps slowly, trying to make no noise. It was dark up there, so he held a flashlight in his left hand. He spanned the attic with the beam of light, seeing nothing. He perched on the top step and waited. He slowly circled the beam of light again. He didn't want to miss up there. All they needed was a hole in the wall from a stray bullet.

And then he saw them. Two shiny eyes staring at him. He raised the gun and braced himself. He didn't like this—didn't like it at all, but he knew his father was counting on him. And he knew his father's hand wasn't steady with a gun—not since he broke two fingers and they weren't set properly. The eyes disappeared and Levi sucked in a breath. Where had the animal gone?

"Son? Anything up there?" his dad whispered.

Levi didn't answer; he was still searching for the varmint. Where had it gone? He heard some scratching movement and swung the gun in that direction. But his flashlight showed nothing.

Levi crawled into the attic and then sat on his haunches, waiting. There. There it was again. The two eyes were looking at him. He could make out the outline of the animal now. He aimed and pressed the trigger. The blast echoed through the attic, reverberating, ringing inside Levi's head. There was a dull thump, and he knew he'd been successful.

It gave him no pleasure, and he hoped the raccoon hadn't been part of a family of raccoons. He didn't want to do this again.

"Did you get it?" Walter asked.

"Did you?" Caleb asked, too. His voice was full of excitement.

"I did," Levi said. "Hopefully, this takes care of the problem."

"At least, for now," Walter said. "Are there anymore up there?"

Levi took a moment to flash the light around the attic again. Nothing. If there were more, they were hiding well.

"*Dat*, can you get a gunnysack for me? I'll bag it and bring it down."

"Let me do it!" cried Caleb. "Can I come up now?"

Levi sighed. "*Jah.* You can come up. But go get me my gloves first. I don't want to be touching the animal. You never know what it might carry."

"Okay. I'll be right back." Caleb paused. "Can I take the gun for you, Levi? Put it back away for you?"

"*Nee*, you can't. Didn't you hear *Dat*? You're not old enough to be handling it yet."

"Fine," Caleb said with consternation. "I'll go get your gloves and a gunnysack and be right back."

And with that, he ran off.

Annie walked in the side door of the big house. She slipped off her shoes in the washroom and went through to the kitchen. Thelma was stirring something on the stove which smelled heavenly.

"I've got some potato soup coming right up," she said, smiling over at Annie. "It'll be ready in a quick minute."

"What can I do to help?" she asked.

"Get the table set. Debbie will help you."

Debbie was already taking utensils out of the drawer. She looked at Annie and scowled. "I can do it myself."

"Since when do you refuse help with your chores?" Thelma chided.

Little Bobby toddled into the kitchen, sucking on two fingers.

"Hello, Bobby," Annie said, bending over to smile at him.

He raised his arms, and Annie laughed, picking him up. "You're a friendly *boppli*, *ain't so*?" she said softly.

"He likes everyone," Debbie said, clearly wanting to set Annie straight.

"Debbie ... the table," Thelma said.

Annie held Bobby and got down the plates with her free hand. She carried them into the dining area and set them around the table.

"Debbie?"

Debbie looked at Annie. "What?"

"Your *mammi's daadi haus* is real pretty. I'm going to take *gut* care of it."

Debbie's eyes filled with tears, but she didn't say anything.

"Which bedroom did your *mammi* sleep in? I imagine it's the one with the really pretty blue and yellow quilt. Am I right?"

Debbie's tears were ready to spill, and she blinked rapidly. She nodded.

"How about I don't use that bedroom. How about I use the other bedroom? Would that make you feel better about me being out there in your *mammi's* house?"

Debbie's lower lip puckered out and despite her efforts, a few tears ran down her cheeks. Again, she nodded.

"Maybe you'd like to come out and help me after supper," Annie said, disentangling Bobby's hands from the strings of her *kapp*. "You can help me unpack and get all my things organized."

Debbie bit her lower lip, and Annie held her breath.

"All right," Debbie finally said, and Annie smiled.

"Thank you, Debbie. That will be a big help to me."

Debbie shrugged as if she weren't all that interested, but Annie could tell that she'd gone a long way in paving the road for a relationship with the young girl.

After the table was set, Annie stood next to Thelma as she cut up the cornbread.

"Henry told me that Marlene Dienner was doing poorly. What's the matter?"

"*Ach*, poor child," Thelma said. "She's in constant pain."

"Constant pain?"

"Her *mamm* told me it's a type of arthritis. Sometimes, her knees will swell up like watermelons."

"*Ach*, that sounds terrible."

"She's laid up a *gut* share of the time. I feel right sorry for her."

"Has she been to an *Englisch* doctor?"

"She has. And Old Mae has seen to her, too. The medicine helps a *gut* bit. But this cold weather doesn't do her any favors."

"Would you mind if I went to see her?"

Thelma turned to her. "*Ach*, child, you don't need my permission to go calling. Just check with Henry to make sure he don't need the buggy."

"Thank you, Thelma."

"Tomorrow, after we work at the toy shop, we can drop you off at Marlene's. I'm sure one of her brothers will bring you home."

"Thank you. I'd like that."

Chapter Five

The next morning, Annie was ready well before breakfast time. Thelma had told her that she could take as many meals with them at the big house as she wished. Of course, she was free to cook for herself in the *daadi haus* if she chose to. But Annie didn't have any groceries at all in the *daadi haus*, so until that was remedied, she would eat in the big house. Not that she minded. She wasn't sure how she would like eating alone. She'd never done it in her entire life, and it sounded lonely.

She was nervous. Today, she would find out exactly what she'd be doing in the toy store. She wanted to do a good job at it, whatever it was. She was grateful for this opportunity, grateful to have family that welcomed her help.

Grateful to be out of Linder Creek, where she might run into Matthew and Doris at any turn.

What was Matthew doing that day? What was he doing right now? Likely going out to the barn to help Nathaniel with the animals.

No. No. No. *Quit thinking about Matthew.* She sucked in a long breath. He wasn't part of her life anymore. He didn't belong to her.

And it was all right. It was. God had a plan for her life, and she must please Him by being faithful to Him, by trusting Him. This was a new beginning for her. A new year and a new beginning. She sent up a prayer of gratitude and then put on her cloak and scarf. She'd run up to the big house now and see if she could help Thelma. No reason to sit around all by herself in the *daadi haus*.

The noises in the attic had stopped since the day before. Both Levi and his father were fairly certain that there had been only one raccoon up there, but that one critter had done a lot of damage. Once Levi had removed the carcass, he and his father had gotten to work. They'd swept up and disposed of the chewed insulation, patched the underside of the roof, and then—despite his mother's fears—Levi had climbed up on the roof and replaced the chewed shingles. In truth, Levi had been as nervous as his mother. The roof was slippery in spots with ice, but it had to be done.

That, or more damage. Already, the urine from the raccoon

had started to seep into the ceiling. It was a mess. Levi and Walter had spent a good part of the day before cleaning it all up. Levi prayed no other raccoons would get it into their heads to move in.

Walter greeted him in the kitchen. "I been thinking," he said. "And I believe I know how to stop them varmints from getting in again."

"Do you?" Levi asked.

"That oak tree," he said, running his thumbs beneath his suspenders. "There's one branch that's grown right close to the roof. I bet that raccoon climbed on it and got to the roof where he promptly started chewing his way through."

Levi's brow rose. "I reckon you're right, at that."

"After breakfast, I think we better go on out there and saw it off."

Caleb walked over to his dad. "I can help with that."

"*Jah*, you can, son. You can hold the ladder for your brother."

Caleb's face fell. "But I'm smaller. I could climb right out on that branch and cut it off. Don't even need no ladder."

"You're gonna fall," seven-year-old Jodie piped up. "'Member that time you fell off the shed when you was climbing?"

Walter's brow shot up. "You fell off the shed?"

"Jodie," Caleb cried at his sister. "You wasn't supposed to tell. You promised."

Jodie's eyes grew huge, and she clapped a hand over her mouth. "Oops."

"When were you climbing on the shed?" Walter asked.

"Long time ago, *Dat*. And I never got hurt. Jodie just had to open her big fat mouth."

"What's this?" Leah asked, entering the kitchen. "What's all this fussing about?"

"Nothing, *Mamm*," Caleb said, giving Jodie a dirty look.

"Since you all have nothing to do but stand around and argue, how about setting the table? How about getting the milk poured?"

Levi chuckled. "All right, *Mamm*. We'll help."

"Sorry, Caleb," Jodie said, tugging on his sleeve. "I never meant to tell."

Caleb scowled, but then he gave her a playful jab in the ribs. She giggled and jabbed him back.

"You two," Leah said, her voice stern but her eyes dancing. "Get the glasses and the milk, will you?"

"*Jah, Mamm*," Caleb and Jodie said at the same time. Then they burst into laughter and pushed at each other to see who could get the glasses first.

~

The toy store was located in Hollybrook, next to the drug store. Annie remembered going into it when she was younger. It was a marvel—a wonderland—of delights. She remembered walking through, running her fingertips along the shelves as she gaped at so many toys all in the same place. There were wooden toys of all varieties, from trucks, to miniature barns, to carved animals. There were dolls, some without faces, and some with button eyes. There were paper kites and board games.

Annie felt the same wonder, looking at it all now. Except that some of the shelves were a bit bare.

"We need to get the new inventory out," Henry told her. "We did well this Christmas. Right well, for which we are grateful. It'll slow down some, now, but folks seem to have taken to these old-fashioned toys." He laughed. "That's what *Englisch* folks call them. Old-fashioned. We just call them toys."

Annie laughed with him. "I'm glad they're popular, *Onkel*."

"We've started shipping them to customers around the state," he told her. "We've got a website up."

She stared at him.

"Now, now, don't you fret. The bishop here has approved computer use for business purposes. We ain't the only ones in the district to use one." He stepped closer to her. "You can learn how, if you want. We could use your help with taking the orders and organizing the shipping."

Her eyes widened. There certainly hadn't been any mention of her using a computer. She wondered how her folks would feel about that. But if the bishop approved it...

"If you'd rather not, I understand," he went on. "We have plenty of other things you can do."

"*Nee*," she said, pensively. "I think I'd like to learn the computer..."

He smiled. "So be it, then. Thelma is pretty *gut* at it, but truth be told, she can't be here every day. The *kinner* need tending and when she brings them to the shop... Well, the toys get spread all over the floor, and it's a distraction to our customers."

"I can imagine it is."

"She enjoys it though, when she is free to come in. We've thought about getting some help to watch the *kinner*, but Thelma ain't too keen on the idea."

"I'll do whatever is most helpful," Annie said. "You just tell me."

"*Gut*." He stood and his eyes scanned the store, and Annie could tell that he was really proud of it. "We have local folks that bring in toys. It helps them make some money while helping the business at the same time. Being winter, we get a lot more as there ain't much to do in the fields. I'll show you how to keep track of that."

He took her into the small office at the side of the store. He pulled out a ledger and showed her the different pages, one for each person who brought in toys. She scanned the figures, seeing when the toys were bought, and the payout to the supplier.

"We keep records of some things in the computer, but I found out that folks around here prefer me to keep track of their earnings with paper and pencil." He chuckled. "I understand that. I don't agree with it, from a business point of view, but I honor it."

She appreciated that. She'd always been fond of Henry, and she wasn't surprised at his deference to others.

"Now, sit yourself down, and get familiar with the ledger. When you feel *gut* about it, then come into the back room, and I'll have you help restock the shelves."

"All right," she said.

"And Thelma told me that you want to see Marlene today. I'll be happy to drop you off after we close the shop. Or you can take the buggy yourself at lunchtime and go around. Whatever suits."

"I'll let you know," Annie said. "Thank you."

He smiled and left her to it. It didn't take long for her to go through all the pages. Her mind was dizzy with the variety of people who brought things in, but she noticed that some of the pages hadn't been touched in months. Clearly, some folks hadn't brought in anything for a while. Yet, looking at the dates recorded in it, others brought in toys on a schedule.

Her uncle also had regular suppliers that weren't from Hollybrook. She saw them listed; although, their records weren't in the ledger. She imagined they were on the computer. She felt a bubble of excitement just thinking about the computer. She looked at it, sitting on an adjoining part of the desk. The screen was black as it wasn't turned on. She ran her fingers over the keyboard, imagining being able to use it. She wondered how long it would take her to get the hang of it. Likely, a very long time. She'd once gone to the public library in Linder Creek and had used a computer to look up a book. The lady from the front desk had helped her. They'd found the book, but Annie had felt guilty for days after using the computer.

But this would be different. This was her job—and the bishop approved.

She grinned. What would Matthew think if he knew she was learning the computer?

She was just scolding herself for such a thought when a thin, wiry-looking young man stuck his head into the office. His green eyes widened with surprise.

"*Ach*, you're not Thelma," he said. Then his cheeks flushed. "Well, obviously, you know that."

Annie laughed. "*Jah*. I know that. I'm Annie, Henry's and Thelma's niece."

He took off his felt hat. "Nice to meet you, Annie. I'm Samuel Hertz."

"Nice to meet you, too. Can I help you?"

Samuel glanced behind him into the store. "I was looking for Thelma or Henry. Henry must be in the back stock room. I've brought my trucks."

"Your trucks...?"

He smiled. "I make toy trucks. I've got two boxes full in my buggy out front."

Annie stood up. "All right. Can you bring them in? And then, you can tell me exactly how many there are, and I'll enter them in the ledger for you."

"Sounds fine." Samuel hesitated a moment, studying her. "You haven't been in Hollybrook long, have you? I would have remembered you."

She blinked, flustered. "*Nee*. Not long."

"I look forward to getting to know you better."

Goodness, but he was forward. Strangely, though, she found she didn't mind it. He smiled at her again and left.

Annie raised a brow, watching him leave. He seemed nice. And he had no beard, so he was single. And by his behavior, she didn't think he was courting anyone.

She blanched. What in the world was she doing? Her face went hot, and she hurriedly flipped through the pages of the ledger to distract herself. She found the page labeled: Samuel Hertz. It appeared that he brought in toy trucks every three months, except right before Christmas, when he brought in an extra supply. He was a regular supplier, then.

She stood at the door of the office and watched as he brought in first one box and then the second. They looked heavy, but he handled them easily. He was clearly stronger than he looked. He glanced up to see her watching him, and she stepped back, feeling foolish. She bustled around behind the desk and sat down. He came in.

"There are twenty trucks in each box, so forty altogether. I can make extra if needed, but I'm thinking that since it's after Christmas, there probably won't be a need for more till my regular delivery in March."

"I'll write down forty trucks." She carefully entered the information in the ledger, and since he hadn't left, she looked back up at him. "*Onkel* told me that they're selling toys to other stores in the state, so there might be a need for more. I'm not sure."

"Ah, so he did start sending them out, then. He was telling me about the possibility." His eyes were warm and friendly.

"So, you're a toy maker," she said.

He laughed. "Only in my spare time. *Dat* keeps me busy out in the fields for most of the year."

She smiled, feeling more at ease with him. "It says here that you're owed a payment. I, well, I don't know how *Onkel* handles that."

"He pays me cash, usually." He nodded toward the desk. "He's got a lock box in the bottom drawer."

Annie pulled out the bottom drawer, and sure enough, there it was. "I'll go find *Onkel* and ask him about it."

Samuel nodded. "I'll wait. No hurry."

She brushed past him as she left the office. She could feel him watching her and it made her feel ungainly, almost as if she couldn't walk properly. How absolutely ridiculous. Was she so desperate after being rejected by Matthew that she grasped onto any man's attention? Was that what this was?

She found Henry in the back room and told him that Samuel Hertz was there. Henry handed her the dolls he'd been holding. "Can you find the spot for these on the shelf? They belong right under the toy trains." And with that, he left to see to Samuel.

Chapter Six

Annie took the buggy at noon and went to Marlene's house. She remembered easily where Marlene lived, which surprised her a bit since she hadn't been there for a few years, and things seemed different. Maybe it was because she hadn't driven a buggy when she'd been there last. In truth, she'd never driven a buggy in Hollybrook.

She remembered how friendly Marlene had been to her. Annie and she had become fast friends, spending every minute together when Annie visited. Once, Marlene had come to Linder Creek. Annie had loved having her there, and had taken her all over, showing her everything and introducing her to everyone.

Again, Annie wondered why they hadn't kept in touch. It was a shame was what it was.

She drove right up to the front porch, feeling a bit ridiculous for showing up at mealtime. But she hadn't wanted to wait until later that day. She secured the reins and then got out of the buggy and went to the door. She knocked and waited.

Within minutes, Marlene's mother answered the door. "Hello. Goodness, but is that you, Annie?"

Annie grinned at her. "Hello, Janet."

Janet Dienner stepped back and ushered her in. "Get on in here. Why, I didn't know you were in town. You visiting?"

"I've come to stay awhile. I'm helping *Aenti* Thelma and *Onkel* Henry at their toy store."

"Well, isn't that nice. *Ach,* but Marlene will be happy to see you."

Annie peered around Janet, looking for Marlene.

Janet's expression sobered. "She ain't down here, Annie. She's up in bed with a bad spell of her arthritis. But you can go right up. She'll be awful pleased to see you."

Annie chewed her lower lip. "If you're sure..."

"Of course, I'm sure. Are you hungry? I've already taken Marlene up her plate. I can make one for you, and you can eat up there together."

Eat in the bedroom? That was unheard of in Annie's family,

but she didn't want to appear rude. And in truth, she was hungry.

"Thank you. That'd be nice," she said.

"And be sure to say hello to Marlene's *dat* and sisters before you leave."

"I will. Thank you."

She scurried up the stairs then, wondering how bad Marlene was that she couldn't join the family for dinner. She went to the second door on the left and knocked gently. It wasn't tightly closed, and it easily opened further when she knocked.

Marlene was lying on her back with a very flat pillow under her head. The quilt covering her looking strange—almost as if it were suspended over her. Marlene's hair was pulled back, though she wore no head covering. Without moving her head, she glanced over at the door. Her brows rose, and her mouth fell open.

"Annie? Is that you?"

Annie rushed into the room, straight to the bed. "Hello, Marlene. *Jah*, it's me."

"*Ach*, but what are you doing here? Did *Mamm* write to you?"

"*Nee.* I'm in town to help out at the toy store, and I was eager to see you."

Marlene's eyes filled with tears and one tear made its way slowly down her cheek. She made no effort to brush it away.

"I bet you never expected to find me in bed."

Annie forced back her own tears. "*Nee,* I didn't. And getting served dinner in bed. Why, it's almost like you're royalty."

Marlene gave a rueful chuckle. "Not hardly, Annie."

Annie pulled a wooden chair up to the bed and sat down. "*Ach*. I'm so sorry."

Marlene tilted her head. "Me, too. But there's nothing for it, but to wait it out. I'm not always laid up in bed. Just when I have the worst spells."

Annie glanced over at the plate of untouched food on her bedside table. "Can I help you?"

"I'm just gathering the courage to try to sit up," Marlene said. "I have to admit, it hurts something fierce."

"I can help you."

Marlene took a deep breath. "All right." She nodded to the rocker in the corner holding a stack of pillows. "I'll need a few of those pillows behind my back."

Annie jumped up and got them. "Tell me what to do."

Marlene was already gritting her teeth. She eased her torso up by pressing her hands on the bed. "Now. Put them behind me now."

Annie squished the pillows behind Marlene and then plumped them about until they looked more comfortable.

"Can you adjust the quilt? It's resting on stacks of towels so that it doesn't come into contact with my right knee."

"Your right knee?"

"It's swollen as big as a bale of hay."

"*Ach.* That sounds awful."

"It *is* awful. There, move the quilt a little. *Jah*. Like that. Thank you." Marlene closed her eyes for a moment and Annie saw the pain on her face. But it cleared somewhat, and Marlene looked at her and smiled. "How long are you staying in Hollybrook?"

"I don't know..."

"I'm right glad you're here, Annie." They gazed at each other, both of them smiling.

"Remind me why we quit writing," Annie said.

Marlene laughed. "I have no idea. Why did we?"

Annie shrugged. "No idea. But it seems silly now."

"It does. *Ach,* but I'm glad you're here."

Janet Dienner came into the room. "Oh *gut*," she said, looking at Marlene. "You're sitting up."

"Annie helped me."

Janet handed Annie a heaping plate of meatloaf, mashed potatoes, green peas, and a thick slice of homemade bread. "Here you are, honey. And here's a glass of milk."

"This looks delicious. Thank you."

Marlene laughed. "I guess my bedroom has become a diner."

"I guess it has," Janet said, looking pleased to see her daughter laughing. "Annie, you stay as long as you like."

"I can't stay too long," Annie said. "*Onkel* will expect me back at the shop soon, but I'll stay as long as I can."

"And come back often," Janet said. She smiled at them both and left the room.

"She worries," Marlene mumbled.

"I imagine she does."

"There ain't a thing she can do. I think that's what bothers her the most."

"But you have medicine?"

"I do. And herbs from Old Mae. They help some, but not a lot." Marlene sighed. "And the medicine costs a fortune. I don't want to take it because of the cost, but I get desperate. My whole body hurts, Annie. Sometimes I can hardly breathe."

"I'm so sorry."

Marlene reached over and took her plate of food from the bedside table. She grunted when she did so, and Annie knew that even that movement hurt her. Annie began eating from her own plate as she watched Marlene balance her plate without letting it touch her lap.

"Do you need help?" Annie asked.

"I always need help," Marlene said with a sigh. "And it gets right tiresome." And then she put on a smile. "Enough about me. Tell me about yourself. What's been happening in Linder Creek? Did you leave behind a beau?"

Annie swallowed her bite of meatloaf. She blinked and set down her fork on her plate.

"Uh oh," Marlene said. "What happened?"

"I was engaged..."

"Engaged? That's wonderful! Wait. *Was* engaged?"

"Matthew and I were engaged for less than a day. We'd been courting for longer, of course. But the morning after we got engaged, he broke it off. He's in love with his cousin—who isn't really his cousin. At least, not by blood." Annie sighed. She'd neglected to mention that she had agreed to marry him when he hadn't even asked—that was simply too humiliating to admit.

"*Ach*, Annie. I'm so sorry. *Gut* riddance, then, right?"

Good riddance? To Matthew? No. Not really.

"*Jah*, I s'pose," she mumbled.

"Now you can meet someone new, *ain't so?*"

Marlene looked so hopeful that Annie couldn't help but smile and agree. "How about you, Marlene? Do you have a beau?"

Marlene's cheeks colored. "You wouldn't think so, would you? Not with my problems. But I do. I have a sweet, loving beau." She frowned. "Is it all right to say that? Or am I making you feel bad?"

"*Nee*, it's fine. Tell me about him."

"He's a farmer, but that's not all he does." Marlene took a small bite of mashed potatoes and swallowed before continuing. "He makes toys. For your *aenti* and *onkel*. Trucks. Annie, they're the cutest trucks ever. I know that little boys are enjoying them so much."

"Trucks?" Annie asked, her eyes widening. Could it be...? It had to be. How many toy truck suppliers could her aunt and uncle have?

"You'll likely meet him one of these days."

"What's his name?" Annie asked, bracing herself for Marlene's answer.

"Samuel Hertz."

Annie pasted on a smile as best she could. Samuel Hertz. The same Samuel Hertz who was flirting with her that very morning? Because he *had* been flirting with her. Had she flirted back? *Ach,* but she hoped not.

"I-I met him."

Despite her discomfort, Marlene's eyes gleamed. "Did you? What did you think? Did you see his trucks? Aren't they clever?"

Annie nodded. "He seemed right nice," she answered. "And *jah*, his trucks are clever."

Marlene shook her head. "I'm sorry. I'm going on about him too much. But I can't talk to anyone else about him. It's not done, you know. Except that *Mamm* and *Dat* do know he's courting me. Because of my... condition, I can't always sneak out for a buggy ride." She gave a rueful laugh. "So, he comes to see me here. Not up in my bedroom, of course. Sometimes, *Mamm* makes a bed for me in the front room. On the davenport."

"That's nice," Annie muttered, her anger for Samuel Hertz growing. How could he be courting Marlene and then act like he had with her? Or had she misunderstood? She wasn't exactly at her most rational these days. Surely, she'd misconstrued his attention, and the very idea was mortifying.

"I was supposed to see him this evening, but now..." Marlene sighed. "Maybe he'll come to the house when I'm not out there to meet him. Or maybe not. He doesn't always come up to the house." She looked at Annie. "Could you take a message to him for me?"

"What? Me?"

"*Jah*, you could tell him that I'm not doing well today and ask him to come early to see me here. I'll ask *Dat* to help me down the stairs."

"But I don't even know him. And I have no idea where he lives." Annie was horrified at the suggestion. "And I can't go right up to his house when he's practically a stranger."

Marlene frowned. "You're right. *Jah.* Of course, you're right. What was I thinking? I'm sorry."

Inwardly, Annie groaned, feeling like a heel. "And I'm sorry for reacting. I s'pose I could go to his farmhouse."

"You likely wouldn't have to," Marlene said.

"What do you mean?"

Marlene glanced at the small wind-up clock on her bedside table. "Sam often has lunch at the diner in town. He might be there now. It's not that far from your toy shop."

"I'll go by on my way back to the shop. If he's there, I'll give him the message."

"*Ach,* thank you so much, Annie. Thank you."

"You're welcome," Annie answered, but her heart felt heavy. Did Marlene know how Samuel acted with other *maidels*?

"Now, let's finish eating," Marlene said, and took another bite of mashed potatoes.

Chapter Seven

Annie gave her greetings to the rest of Marlene's family before she left, and she also promised Marlene's mother that she'd be back soon.

"You did her a world of *gut*," Janet Dienner told her as she was showing her out. "I could see it on her face. Thank you for coming."

"You're welcome. I enjoyed seeing all of you again," Annie said. She left the house and got into the buggy. She wished she hadn't told Marlene that she'd try to find Samuel at the diner. Yet on the other hand, she was glad to help Marlene in any way she could. What must it be like to be in such pain? What must it be like to not be able to get around freely?

Annie felt humbled. Here she'd been consumed with her own heartbreak and there were people all around her with much more serious concerns. For the first time in days, she caught a true glimpse of the depth of her own blessings.

As she got closer to the toy shop, Annie studied the businesses, looking for the diner. She easily spotted it and pulled over to the side of the road, where gratefully, there were two parallel parking spots big enough for the horse and buggy. She secured the reins and got out, wanting to make this quick. She entered the diner to the tinkle of the bells above the door. She scanned the tables inside and saw Samuel, eating a large hamburger.

She squared her shoulders and walked over to him. He looked up and did a double take.

"Annie? I didn't expect to see you here." When she didn't immediately answer, he pulled out the chair at the side of his table. "Sit down. Did I forget something at the shop?"

Annie didn't want to sit down, but neither did she want to stand there in the middle of the diner. She sat. "*Nee*, you didn't forget anything."

"Oh." He smiled. "Did you just see me in passing then?"

She shook her head. "*Nee.* Marlene sent me."

That bit of news shocked him. "What is it?" he asked. "What's happened?"

"She's having a bad spell and wanted me to let you know."

His forehead creased. "*Ach.* Not again."

"She wondered if you might want to stop by and come up to the house..."

He nodded slowly. "I can do that." He slumped a bit in his chair. "Is she in a lot of pain?"

"*Jah*."

His frown deepened. "How do you know her?"

"I've known her for a *gut* while. We used to play together as children. I'd lost touch, though, which I regret." Annie was studying him. He seemed to be genuinely disturbed at the news. So, Annie had been wrong. He hadn't been flirting with her.

He rubbed his hand over his chin. "Hopefully, this spell won't last long. She gets them often, you know. Once or twice a month."

"For how long? I mean, when we were younger, she didn't have this condition."

He shrugged. "It's only been the last few years." He gazed at her. "I didn't know... I mean, I wasn't aware it was this bad."

"But you're courting her."

"Only for the last six months or so. I, well, I didn't realize it was this bad until recently. She tries to cover it up..."

Annie could understand that. She wouldn't want people peering at her with pity all the time—and they would. Of course, they would. Folks in communities like theirs were full of compassion.

"But you're still courting her."

Samuel blinked as if surprised by her comment. "I... Well, what kind of a person would I be if I broke up with her when I found out?" His words were touching, but there was something beneath them that made Annie a bit uncomfortable. She couldn't really pinpoint what it was exactly. And then she wondered whether her recent experience with Matthew was coloring her opinion or making her suspicious when there was no call for it.

"I better go," she murmured and stood up.

He touched her arm. "Thank you for letting me know."

She glanced down at his fingers on her arm. Of course, she had on her cloak, but still, it seemed a bit forward considering they didn't know each other. "You're welcome."

He'd noticed her gaze, and he dropped his hand. "I'll be seeing you around."

"*Jah*," she said. "*Gut*-bye, Samuel."

"*Gut*-bye."

Caleb Swarey eyed the pistol his brother used to shoot the

raccoon the other day. It was on the top shelf of the cabinet in the hallway. In truth, Caleb couldn't quite reach the gun, but he wanted to. He was sure there was a fat rat in the barn. He'd seen evidence of it just the other morning. One of the sacks of chicken feed had been chewed through, leaving a mess. He hadn't told his dad about it—he wanted to handle it himself.

If he could snatch the gun and go out to the barn, he could shoot it. Levi didn't like to use the gun, so likely he'd be right glad if Caleb took care of it himself. Well probably at first, Levi and his dad would be upset with him, but then they'd be grateful.

And how hard could it be to use the gun, anyway? He'd watched his dad more than once, and Levi, too. Caleb grinned, the idea becoming more enticing by the minute. He listened carefully. He heard Jodie talking with their mother in the kitchen. And Levi and his dad had gone into town to the Feed & Supply. They wouldn't be back for an hour, at least.

He bit his bottom lip and decided to do it. With quick, quiet movements, he fetched the footstool from the bathroom and brought it out to the hallway. He climbed up and easily retrieved the gun. He also picked up the box of bullets stored at the very back of the shelf. He took out a handful and replaced the box. Then he got down, put the stool away, and stuck the gun inside his shirt. He closed his fist around the bullets, feeling the cool pieces of metal dig into his palm. His heart was beating wildly with excitement.

He was about to have his first shoot.

Unfortunately, he had to walk through the kitchen to get to his coat and boots. But when he stepped into the room, his mother and Jodie were so busy frosting a cake, they barely looked up. He slipped right on through, and once he'd cleared their line of vision, he called out, "*Mamm*, I'm going out to the barn to see to the animals."

His mother barely grunted in reply.

Smiling widely now, he put on his coat and boots and burst outside into the frigid January air. He crunched across the yard and entered the barn. He decided to leave the door wide open, despite the cold. Otherwise, it would be just too dark to see his prey. He sat on a bale of hay and loaded the gun, grateful that he had a keen eye when he'd watched his dad do the same thing.

He set the gun on the bale of hay and then walked over to the sack of chicken feed. He reached inside and grabbed a handful. Then he spread it out on the ground as bait. Now, what rat would be able to resist that? He chuckled at the thought. Then he went back and arranged the bales of hay, hiding behind them. He left a window of sorts, though, so he could stick his hand with the gun through to get a good shot.

And then he settled in to wait. Rats liked to be out and about mostly at night, but Caleb figured that it was fairly dark in the barn, so surely, the critter would be making his appearance soon. He listened with all his might as he tried to make himself comfortable. If he didn't get the rat this time, he'd come back out later when his dad was busy with something else. Goodness, but his dad would be proud of him for taking this on.

One of the cows kicked against his stall, and Caleb jerked, nearly squeezing the trigger in surprise. When he realized it was just old Bertha, he laughed to himself. He was a bit jumpy. He heard some rustling noise and his pulse quickened, but again, it was Bertha.

"Stay still," he muttered to the cow. "You're getting me too nervous."

The minutes ticked by, and Caleb was getting stiff, staying in his awkward position. He shifted, trying not to make any noise. He peered through his little window, but the chicken feed was undisturbed. He sighed. This was a boring, but he couldn't give up so quick-like.

And then he heard it. A noise at the barn door. Was it the rat? He couldn't quite see from his vantage point. His hand tightened on the gun and a bead of sweat covered his upper lip.

"Caleb?"

Caleb groaned. It was Jodie, of all things.

"What do you want?" he called from his hiding spot.

"Where are you?" she asked. "*Mamm* wants to know if you're hungry."

"I ain't hungry. Now go back inside."

"Where are you?" she asked again. Caleb heard her wondering about, looking for him.

He stood up. "I'm right here. Now, go back inside."

"What are you doin' back there?"

"None of your business. Go back on in."

She scowled. "I ain't going back in till you tell me what you're doing." She walked toward him and then her boots started to crunch on the scattered chicken feed. She looked down. "*Ach*, what a mess. How come there's chicken seeds all over the floor in here?"

Caleb blew out his breath in frustration. "Because I'm setting a trap."

"For the chickens?" she asked. "What for?"

"*Nee*, not for the chickens. For a rat."

She froze. "A rat? There's a rat?"

"*Jah*," he said, seeing his advantage. "Now, go on in." But he made a mistake and raised his right hand. Jodie's gaze immediately glommed onto the gun.

"What are you goin' to do with the gun?" Her eyes went huge. "Are you goin' to shoot the rat?"

"None of your business," he cried, lowering his hand. "Now, go on."

But Jodie wasn't about to leave now. She hurried over to him and crawled over the bales of hay. There was barely enough room for both of them in his hiding spot.

"I want to shoot the rat, too," she announced. "I don't like 'em."

"Guns ain't for girls," Caleb said, feeling his importance. "Men do the shooting."

"You ain't no man," she said and laughed.

It was the laugh that did it. Caleb drew himself up to his full height and raised his chin. "I am so. I got this gun, don't I?" He raised his hand again, and then to his horror, his finger moved on the trigger. Later, he wouldn't be able to explain it. He had no idea why his finger closed on that piece of waiting metal. Or how.

But the blast roared through the barn, nearly deafening him. Jodie's eyes went wide with terror and then she curled in on herself and crumpled against him sliding to the ground.

What had happened? Had he *shot her?*

"*Nee!*" he shrieked. In terror, he dropped the gun. And then he knelt by his sister. Her eyes were closed, and she was still. He screamed and hefted up her head and shoulders, cradling her on his lap. "Jodie? Jodie? Wake UP! *NEE!*"

And then everything broke loose. He heard the door to the house slam shut, and he heard his mother race into the barn.

"What's happened!" she cried. "I heard a gun!"

Caleb was crying now, rocking his sister's body in his lap. "I didn't mean to do it, *Mamm*. I didn't. I didn't mean it!" He was going to vomit. The bile surged up his throat. He coughed and choked and couldn't take his eyes off his sister's still face.

His mother climbed her way around the hay and when she beheld her daughter on Caleb's lap, she screamed, "JODIE!" She kicked aside a bale of hay and dropped to her knees. She felt over Jodie's body and her hand came away covered in blood. "*Nee! Nee! Nee!*"

"*Mamm*, is she... *Mamm? Mamm!*"

"Run to the phone shanty," his mother ordered. "NOW! Call 911! GO!" She took Jodie into her lap.

Caleb scrambled up, crying, coughing, and choking. He stumbled from the barn. When he emerged, tearing across the frozen ground, he could barely see for his tears.

"911.. 911..." he hollered, but there was no one to hear him. The phone shanty was a stone's throw from the end of their drive. He lunged toward it, grabbing the door and throwing it open. He dialed and quickly told the operator where they were located. He threw the receiver down and hurtled back across the street.

He saw the buggy coming then. His dad and Levi. His knees buckled, and he went down on the road. The buggy drew up short beside him.

"Son!" Walter cried, jumping from the buggy.

Levi was quick to follow. "Caleb! Are you hurt?"

Caleb looked at them through a dark tunnel. He blinked and sobbed. "It's.. It's Jodie. She's hurt. The barn..."

He got no further. His father and brother went tearing up the drive. Caleb got up, his legs shaking so badly, he could barely move. He grabbed Clipper's bridle and made his way back to the barn.

Chapter Eight

Levi gasped in horror. There was a pool of blood on Jodie's stomach. His mother was holding her hand over the wound, blood seeping through her fingers.

"What happened?" Walter yelled.

"She's been shot," Leah managed to sputter.

Never in his life had Levi seen such a look of raw terror on his mother's face. His stomach lurched. Shot? Jodie had been *shot?* How in the world—

Walter was leaning over her now. He gently pulled his wife's hand from the wound. He gasped and pressed it back on it.

"The a-ambulance..." Leah stuttered. "It's c-coming."

And then Levi heard the siren, wailing and getting closer and closer. He ran out of the barn to direct them. He raced to the road and saw the vehicle immediately. He waved both arms over his head, and the ambulance blasted into the yard. It screeched to a halt and the two medics hurried out, one getting the gurney.

"Here!" Levi called. "In the barn."

The men rushed past him. Levi followed them inside. Within minutes, Jodie was on the gurney, and they were getting her inside the ambulance. Leah and Walter climbed into the back with her.

"Tell Bishop!" Walter cried as the door closed on him.

The siren wailed again as the ambulance pulled out. Levi felt weak, his stomach churned. And then he saw his brother. Caleb was curled into a ball by the side of the barn. Another siren sounded and Levi turned to see a police car coming up the drive. It also screeched to a halt, and an officer jumped out.

Caleb had covered his head with his hands and was sobbing. Levi hurried to him, kneeling by his side.

"What happened, Caleb? Did you see it? Did Jodie shoot herself? How did she get the gun?"

Caleb couldn't speak; he just looked up at Levi with huge eyes full of terror. He shook his head over and over. The policeman approached and Levi stood up.

"I need to know what happened," he said.

Levi looked down at his brother. "My sister was shot. I-I don't know how. My brother will tell us."

Levi reached down to help Caleb up, but Caleb resisted him. Finally, he said, "Caleb. Stand up. Stand up now. It's going to be all right. You need to tell the officer what happened."

Caleb got up and what happened spilled from his mouth.

"We're closing shop now!" Henry told Annie. "Get into the buggy. Hurry!"

"What's happened?" Annie asked, scuttling around the desk and grabbing her cape from its peg. She heard the urgency in her uncle's voice, but he was already across the shop, flipping the sign from Open to Closed.

"Quick-like!" he cried.

She dashed outside and got into the buggy. It was already hitched up, which she thought odd. What had happened? Was something wrong with one of the children? But then she noticed two other buggies going down the road at a good clip.

"There's been a shooting," Henry told her, climbing inside the buggy. It sagged a bit with his weight. He picked up the reins, clicked his tongue and they were underway, following the other two buggies. "We're going to the hospital."

"A ... shooting?" Annie asked, her stomach churning. "Is it... Is it...?"

"*Nee*. Not one of ours. It's the Swarey girl. Jodie Swarey. She's about seven or eight..."

"A shooting? Did someone *shoot her?*" Annie clasped a hand to her chest.

"I don't know. We'll find out."

It took about ten minutes to get to the hospital. Henry drove the wagon to the area designated specifically for buggies and horses. Annie counted five already there, and one pony cart. *Ach*, but who was driving an open pony cart in this cold? Henry parked the buggy, secured the reins, and they both got out. Annie had to stretch her gait to keep up with her uncle. Once inside, they were directed to the emergency waiting room. It was full of Amish folks. Annie knew hardly anyone, so she moved to the outskirts of the crowd.

There was an eerie silence in the crowded room, broken only by the sounds of a woman's occasional sobs. Annie was certain that the woman had to the be girl's mother. A man had his arm around her, and there was a terrified looking boy sitting stiffly on the end of the couch. A brother, maybe? Annie scanned the faces of everyone there. The fear in the room crept inside her, and she sent up prayers for the little girl.

A young man, likely about her age, paced the corner of the room.

His face was grim, and she could see the anxiety in his every step. Another brother, perhaps? He must have felt her watching him. He glanced at her and their eyes locked for a brief, tense moment, and then he looked away and continued pacing.

She could see some people's eyes closed, and she knew they were praying—just as she was. Henry went right over to the crying woman and her husband. He spoke to them for a few minutes and then came over to stand beside her.

"It was an accident," he murmured close to Annie's ear. "Her brother. It was an accident."

Oh, dearest Lord. Jodie's brother had shot her? Her eyes flew to the boy sitting on the couch. He had no color in his cheeks. His eyes were sunken, and he looked ready to vomit. It had to have been him. Her heart went out to him. How horrifying to have accidentally shot your sister. She couldn't fathom what he must be feeling.

Their wait stretched out. Every minute that passed seemed to increase the tension in the room. Annie wished she could do something, *anything*, to help. She could pray. That was all, and God willing, it would be enough. The girl's mother had now slumped against the father. Her eyes were shut tightly, and her lips moved silently.

Annie heard a few words here and there from others who were waiting, so she knew Jodie was in surgery. From what Annie could surmise, the girl had been shot in the stomach.

Annie looked up as the young man who had been pacing drew near.

"Who are you?" he asked. Under other circumstances, his words might have sounded rude and abrupt, but Annie knew he was distracting himself by talking to her.

"I'm Annie Hershberger. I'm Henry's and Thelma's niece from Linder Creek."

He attempted a smile, but it didn't happen. "Nice to meet you. I'm Levi Swarey."

So, it was another brother. "I-I'm so sorry about your sister."

His eyes filled with tears, and he nodded. Then he visibly swallowed and asked, "Are you visiting?"

"*Nee*. I'm here for a while. I'm working in the toy shop."

He nodded again. "I see." He licked his lips and rubbed his hands down his trousers. He glanced over at the door where a doctor or nurse would eventually emerge to give them news. He looked back at her. "So, what will you be doing at the shop?"

They began to chat, unimportant things—things that really didn't matter at all in light of what was happening. But Annie kept the conversation going, knowing it was a help to him.

"I'll be learning the computer," she added and then wished she hadn't. Computer use was a highly controversial subject—

even with the bishop's approval for business use. She didn't want to upset Levi further.

But he seemed not to mind. Or notice much, either. His eyes kept flicking toward the door.

"We should hear soon," she said, hopping to ease his mind. But she didn't know that. Was it good news that it was taking so long? Or bad news? She had no idea. But the longer it went without someone coming out, the longer little Jodie was hanging on.

"That's what I keep thinking," Levi replied. He stopped fidgeting and leaned a bit closer. "Do you... Do you think she'll be all right?"

Annie blanched. She had no idea. She put on a smile. "She must be a fighter," she said. "Or they would have been out sooner."

He nodded. "I was thinking the same thing. So really, no news is *gut* news, *ain't so?*"

"I'm sure it is," she murmured, praying she was right.

"I, uh, I... This is all my fault." The words tumbled from his lips and then he gave her a stunned look, as if wondering why in the world he'd said that out loud. And to her—a virtual stranger.

She blinked. "What?"

"I..." He swallowed again and a look of helplessness covered his face. His eyes were stricken, and he was breathing hard. She knew no one else could hear him, and she was glad. What was he talking about anyway? Had she misunderstood things? Was it he who'd shot the gun? She'd assumed it had to be the younger boy. She must have been wrong.

"I knew my little brother was curious. More than curious. He was itching... He was itching to shoot that gun..."

So it had been the younger brother.

"I should have known. I should have locked it away. I-I put it on the shelf. Like always. I should have known."

His face crumpled, and he covered it with his hands. Annie wanted to put her arms around him. She didn't know him, but she felt his anguish. Felt it to the very bottom of her heart. She wanted to ease it somehow, but what could she do? She remained silent, but she took a half-step closer.

He took his hands away and sniffed. "*Ach*, I'm sorry. You don't know me."

"It doesn't matter," she whispered. "It doesn't matter. I'm so very sorry."

"If I'd only locked it—"

"How could you have known? It was an accident, Levi. A tragic, horrible accident."

"And where was *Gott*?" he asked, his voice barely audible. "Where was *Gott*?"

"Right there with her," she said slowly, her heart aching for him. She didn't want to just spout platitudes, but she believed what she was saying with all her being. "And He's with her right now."

Levi looked at her through his tears, and at that moment, she'd never felt closer to anyone in her life. Her breath caught in her throat, and she was in awe at how a tragedy could make strangers into intimate friends. He gave her an odd, questioning look, and she wondered whether he felt it, too.

"Thank you," he said softly. "For listening."

She nodded, fighting tears herself now.

And then it happened. The swinging door opened, and a doctor walked out. He scanned the crowd until he saw the Swareys. Annie could feel the entire room hold their breath. The doctor neared the waiting parents, who had struggled to their feet. He stepped close, and Annie only made out the low cadence of his voice and then Mrs. Swarey cried out and collapsed in her husband's arms.

Annie went stiff and tears filled her eyes. No. *No.* Levi rushed over to his parents and threw his arms around them. They were all weeping. The younger boy looked like death himself. He slid down onto the floor and curled into a ball. And then Levi seemed to remember him and went down to the floor with him. He cradled him and rocked him back and forth, both of them crying.

Henry came to stand by Annie. "*Ach,* but this is sad news," he said, his voice heavy. "Poor Jodie. Everyone will be heartbroken. Such a pretty, happy little thing. But *Gott* knows best. We have to believe it."

Annie did believe it, but she felt it would be little comfort to the Swareys right then. She couldn't seem to take her eyes off Levi. He was standing now, pulling his brother up with him. The boy didn't have any strength, and Annie could see that Levi was basically holding him upright. The parents reached out to the younger boy, but he went stiff. He was caught up in a hug that looked wooden.

Gott help him, Gott help him, Annie prayed.

"There's nothing more we can do here now," Henry said. "I need to get home and tell Thelma. She's likely heard something by now and will be wondering. *Ach,* this is a sad day."

Annie took one last look at Levi. She gave a start when he looked straight at her. She felt his emotion, his grief slice through her and then he turned away. She caught her breath and scurried to catch up to her uncle.

Chapter Nine

Levi had finally gotten Caleb to bed. The police had questioned them all again before they left the hospital. It had nearly done Caleb in. The poor boy was almost unresponsive by the time they finally got home. The funeral home had made arrangements to come for Jodie's body and would bring it to the house the next day.

Levi sat on the edge of his bed and wondered at how differently the day had ended from how it had started. Just that morning, he'd teased Jodie and tickled her at the breakfast table. Just that morning, he'd listened to her chatting happily with their mother. Just that morning, he'd watched Jodie clear away the dishes like a proper young lady.

He sucked in his breath. *Ah, Jodie. Jodie. Jodie.* When he'd stood by her hospital bed and gazed on her lifeless little face, his throat had nearly closed. She was so still. So quiet. So pale. Caleb wouldn't come close. He hovered at the curtain that hung on metal chains, separating Jodie from other patients who still lived. He wouldn't come in. Levi had tried, his parents had tried, but Caleb's feet were cemented in place, and he wouldn't move.

Levi stood up from his bed and walked to the window, peering out into the cold, dark outdoors. Jodie would never again swing on the tire hanging from the oak tree. She'd never again skip across the yard to see to the chickens. She'd never again...

He squeezed his eyes shut. *Stop. Stop,* he told himself. Surely, Jodie was in heaven now. Surely, God had welcomed her to his kingdom. Surely... Levi gasped in a gulping breath. If only he had locked the gun away. Then Caleb couldn't have gotten it. He couldn't have taken it out to the barn.

Rats? He'd gone out to *shoot rats?*

Levi shook his head, and the tears started down his face again. His brother had wanted to be a hero. He'd wanted to do something helpful.

Levi didn't care if the barn was full of rats—he'd gladly take that if he could have his sister back.

The cold in the room seeped into his bones, and finally, when he was stiff with it, he got into bed and tried to go to sleep.

Annie stayed in the big house that night with the family. She lay in bed, staring up at the dark ceiling. She heard some quiet rustling from the adjoining room and figured that Thelma was in there, seeing to Bobby, who'd been fussy. Supper that evening had been a solemn affair and after *redding* up the kitchen, she and Thelma had made banana bread and a noodle casserole to take over to the Swareys the next day. The toy shop wouldn't open. Once Jodie's body was taken home, there would be a viewing for the rest of the day.

The funeral would likely be the following day.

In two days, Jodie would be buried in the ground and no one would ever see her or hear her or enjoy her again. Three days in total, and it was over. Annie shuddered in bed, pulling the quilts up more firmly under her chin.

Her mind went to Levi, and she wondered how he was doing. How his whole family was doing. Strange, but she'd just experienced the worst broken heart in her entire life when Matthew rejected her. But now, in the light of this tragedy, her broken heart seemed almost inconsequential. She knew it wasn't. It had hurt—and it still hurt. But in comparison, it was nothing.

Her eyes burned with tears. She didn't know Jodie, but she mourned her just the same.

The next day after the noon meal, Thelma herded all the children into the buggy. Annie brought the casserole and the banana bread and climbed into the back with the children. Henry drove, and there was little talk on the way. Annie knew once they arrived, there would be much talking and even much laughter. While sad and often tragic, viewings and funerals were an opportunity to get together, to get caught up, to share gossip. The children would run about the yard playing, only stopping to eat from the bounty of food which would trickle in all day long.

Annie still didn't know many folks in Hollybrook, so she planned to make herself useful in the kitchen. She was sure Mrs. Swarey would be grateful for the help. The Swarey yard was full of buggies when they arrived. Thelma led the children into the house with Annie at their heels. Henry stayed back to see to the horse.

Inside, the house was bulging with folks, and as Annie predicted, she heard thick rumbles of talking and laughing. In the kitchen, women flitted about, arranging the food, pouring coffee, and making tea.

"I'll help in the kitchen," she told Thelma.

"Thank you. I'll pay my respects and then join you shortly."

Annie nodded and immediately got to work washing up the stack of dirty dishes that had already accumulated. She introduced herself to the women, some of whom remembered her from her past visits.

She stood at the sink washing the dishes, gazing through the kitchen window. She recognized Samuel Hertz, who was walking toward the house with what was surely his family. He glanced her way and their eyes met. He smiled and nodded at her and she nodded back and then quickly put her attention to the dishes she was scrubbing.

She didn't know why, but he made her uncomfortable.

"Annie, would you take the pot of coffee into the front room and see if anyone wants a refill?" a hefty red-cheeked woman asked her. Annie couldn't remember her name.

"*Jah*, of course," she agreed, setting the clean dish in the drainer.

"I'll finish these up," the woman said.

Annie took the pot and shimmied her way into the front room which was packed with people. Jodie's casket lay at the front of the room, to the side of the warming stove. It was open and Annie could see the young girl, lying there. Her face was sweet, and Annie could immediately see her resemblance to both Levi and Caleb. Her hair was pulled back tightly, arranged perfectly beneath her *kapp*. She wasn't very big; she must have been slight for her age.

And then Annie spotted Levi. He was standing at the foot of the casket, but his eyes were on her. She smiled. He didn't smile back, but there was something in his look. Gratitude or maybe it was just recognition, but she felt it. Felt something.

He appeared stoic, but she could tell he'd been crying. Without thinking, she moved toward him.

"Do you want some coffee?" she asked, only then realizing that he didn't have a cup nor did she. "Oh. Sorry."

He gazed down at her. "I don't like coffee," he told her. "Jodie always wanted a sip and *Dat* would let her drink a bit. I like the smell just fine, but the taste is bitter."

"Me, too. I mean, I think it's bitter, too."

He gave her a small smile and then looked down at his hands.

"I'm sorry," she whispered.

He nodded but didn't look at her. She was ready to walk away when he touched her arm. His eyes were back on hers. "My-my brother is outside."

"Is he?" Her forehead creased. She wasn't sure what she was supposed to say.

"He won't come in."

"He ... he's upset." Her words were so inadequate and such a gross understatement, that she flinched.

Levi blew out his breath. "Will you come with me?" he asked.

Her eyes widened. This was highly unusual, but she felt such compassion for him that she would have done anything to help.

"Of course," she agreed immediately.

She caught Thelma's eye and went to her and gave her the pot of coffee. And then she slipped out of the room behind Levi. He led her through the washroom, not even bothering to put on his coat. She'd taken off her cloak when they arrived, so she went outside without a wrap, too. He stood on the side porch, glancing around.

"Maybe, he's in the barn," she suggested.

"Maybe."

She had no idea why she was out there with him. She didn't know Caleb. How could she possibly help?

Levi pushed open the barn door and stepped inside. The air was only slightly warmer in there, but at least they were out of the cold breeze. She was shivering now, but she tried to hide it.

"Caleb?" Levi called.

There was no answer. Annie looked around through the afternoon shadows. She thought she saw movement behind the plow that was sitting to the side. Levi looked at her, and she pointed in that direction. Levi strode over and then stopped, looking down.

"Caleb. There you are." Levi squatted. "Come on inside. You must be hungry."

Annie thought she heard a mumbled reply, but she wasn't sure. She could see the boy now, huddled in a ball.

"*Mamm* and *Dat* are worried about you. So am I. Come in, Caleb. Please."

"*Nee*." His voice was louder this time.

Annie didn't move. She was afraid that her presence would actually spook Caleb. Why had Levi asked her to come out there with him, anyway? She closed her eyes and sent up a fervent prayer for Caleb. And Levi. And the whole family.

Levi reached out and pulled Caleb close to him. There was a gasp and then loud sobbing. The sound of anguish slashed through Annie. She began to weep silently for the boy's pain. Levi held him while he cried. Annie saw a folded blanket on a bench. It was likely a horse blanket, but it looked clean. She picked it up and slowly stepped closer to the two brothers. She draped the blanket around Caleb. He didn't even seem to notice, but Levi did. He looked at her with gratitude.

She touched his shoulder and then backed away, leaving the barn. Leaving the brothers to console each other in their anguish.

She stepped back inside the house, going through the washroom. She paused. She was shivering and she wanted to warm up a minute before she joined the crowd.

"Annie."

Annie turned to see Samuel standing in the doorway. "*Ach*, Samuel. You startled me."

"I didn't know you knew Levi."

"I-I don't, really."

"Weren't you just outside with him?"

Annie's brow lowered. "Were you watching me?"

He fumbled a bit, looking uneasy. "*Nee*. Of course, not. I just couldn't help but notice."

"We were looking for Caleb," she said, although she had no idea why she had to justify her actions to him.

"Poor guy," Samuel said, then, his voice sympathetic.

Annie's shoulders relaxed. "I know. He's right upset."

"I can only imagine."

She waited for him to step aside and let her through to the kitchen, but he seemed in no hurry to move.

"Is Marlene here?" Annie asked.

"Marlene? I haven't seen her yet. I don't think she'll be coming. Perhaps her family will come."

"She's still bad, then?"

"She was last evening when I stopped by."

"So, you did stop by?" Annie said, for some reason surprised.

“Of course, I did.”

Annie studied his face, wondering what it was about him that bothered her so. His expression appeared perfectly normal, and he had gone to see Marlene. Annie smiled at him, ashamed of her poor opinion of him.

“Will you be in the store tomorrow?” he asked.

“We’ll be closed for the funeral.”

“*Ach*, of course.” He shook his head. “How silly of me.”

“Why did you want to know?’

“I was thinking of stopping by for a few minutes.”

“What do you need?”

“Oh...” He looked down at his shoes and then back up at her. “I just wanted to check... Well, I wanted to talk to Henry for a moment.”

“He’s here. You can talk to him now.”

Samuel’s face turned a pale shade of red. “Of course. What was I thinking?” And with that, he turned away and left her staring after him.

Samuel Hertz, she thought, *you are a strange person.*

Annie went back into the kitchen and started right in with the dishes again. In the few minutes she’d been gone, there was even more food now weighing down the table. Some people were standing about, helping themselves. Annie looked through the window again and saw both Levi and Caleb emerge from the barn. Levi looked to be almost pulling Caleb along with him. Even from that distance, they both looked cold and forlorn.

Annie quickly went to the stove and poured two cups of tea. When the two of them came in through the washroom, she held out both cups to them.

Levi grasped the tea. "*Ach*, thank you, Annie."

Caleb just stared at her. She thought he might recognize her from the hospital, but she doubted it. He'd been pretty well out of it. But he did take the cup of hot tea, curling his hands around the mug.

"C'mon, Caleb," Levi said gently. "We'll go into the dining area and sit at the table. I'll get you something to eat."

Caleb's eyes filled with tears, but he didn't resist Levi's suggestion. With leaden feet, he followed Levi from the room.

Annie watched them go.

Chapter Ten

Levi stayed by Caleb's side all day. In truth, he wanted to spend more time in the front room, close to Jodie's body. He found a strange sort of comfort there, beside her. But after taking a cursory glance at their sister's body, Caleb wouldn't go into the room again. They spent a good portion of the day sitting at the dining room table. If Caleb would've had his way, he would have spent the day upstairs in bed or back in the barn, but Levi wouldn't let him. He needed to be with their people, needed to see that no one hated him for what had happened. In truth, many folks had come up to Caleb. They didn't say much, but they did pat him on the back. At each touch, Levi saw Caleb wince, but he didn't move or shove their hands away.

By evening, Caleb was pale and slumped. The stricken look

had not left his face the entire day. Finally, everyone had cleared out, ready to return the following morning for the funeral. Caleb looked up at Levi with such a pathetic expression that Levi stood to usher his brother to bed. But before he could, their parents came into the room. All day, they'd been in with Jodie, talking and crying and even laughing a time or two. Levi had kept his eye on them through the doorway. He'd purposely positioned himself at the dining table where he could keep watch.

He'd met his mother's gaze more than once as she peered through the door. He knew she was checking on Caleb, but she never did come in.

But she came in now, with Walter behind her.

She sat down and reached across the table to lay her hand on top of Caleb's. Caleb stiffened and wouldn't meet her gaze.

"How are you doing, son?" she said, her voice low, but steady.

Caleb bit his bottom lip and looked ready to burst into tears all over again.

"I reckon he's exhausted," Walter said, "like the rest of us."

"I was going to take him up to his bedroom," Levi told them.

His mother nodded. "*Gut.* That's *gut.* Get a *gut* night's sleep." She licked her lips and took a deep breath. "Sleep well, Caleb, and we'll see you in the morning."

Caleb nodded, the tears coming now.

"Enough crying, son," Walter said, though not unkindly. "You do what your *mamm* says and get some sleep."

Caleb nodded again, clearly unable to speak. Levi stood and helped him up. The two of them went upstairs. Levi helped him into bed after Caleb mechanically got into his pajamas. It was cold up there. Cold and silent. Levi fancied he could hear his own thoughts echo through the empty room.

"Go to the bathroom, Caleb, and come right back. I'll sit with you a while."

Caleb took the lantern and left the room. Levi eased himself into the straight chair in the corner of the room. He ached all over. How odd. He hadn't done a physical thing all day long, but it felt like he'd worked himself into a lather. Everything muscle hurt. But his heart hurt most of all.

Caleb shuffled back into the room. Levi jumped up and took the lantern, setting it on the bedside table. He threw back the quilts and helped Caleb into bed. Then he covered him up and did something he hadn't done for years and years. He leaned down and kissed Caleb on the cheek. He tasted the boy's tears and nearly began crying himself.

"*Gut* night, Caleb," he whispered. "It'll get better. You'll see."

Caleb turned over and Levi snuffed out the lantern. He went back to the straight chair and sat down. There were no extra quilts sitting about, but he simply didn't have the energy to go get one from his bedroom, so he just sat in the dark and got colder and colder with each minute that passed.

"I can't believe it," Thelma said the next morning. "I can't believe we're preparing to go to a funeral. What a way to start the new year."

"Wife," Henry said, "we have to trust in the *gut* Lord. He knows what He's doing."

"Well, he should have known what that Caleb Swarey was doing two days ago," she snapped back. "And then we'd still have Jodie with us."

"It was her time," Henry said. He sighed. "You need to control your words, Thelma. There are big ears listening to everything you say."

And indeed, there were. All the children, even the youngest, were staring at their mother with wide eyes. Annie went over to where they were all perched on a dining room bench.

"Have you finished your breakfasts?" she asked kindly, taking their attention from Thelma.

"I ain't finished yet," Dale said, forking another bite of eggs.

"You're the slowest eater ever," Debbie observed. "Like a turtle."

"You're a turtle," George chirped. "Dale's a turtle."

"I ain't either!" Dale snapped. "And you ain't done eating either, you big fat turtle."

"*Kinner!*" their father scolded. "That will be enough. All of you finish the food on your plates, and Annie will help you wash up. I want all your teeth brushed and all of you ready to go in twenty minutes. You hear me?"

"*Jah, Dat*," they all mumbled.

When the last bite was taken, Annie shepherded them upstairs to brush their teeth. Thelma had told her that she'd take care of the dishes. Thelma was deeply upset about Jodie's death. From what Annie could tell, Thelma hadn't been all that close to Jodie. But Debbie was the same age as Jodie was, and Annie wondered if Thelma was so affected because of that. It could just as easily have been Debbie who'd been accidentally shot. Annie shuddered. No matter how you thought of it, it was a tragedy.

Did she agree with Henry? Had it been Jodie's time? Annie didn't know. In truth, the thought wasn't much comfort. She supposed it should be, but it wasn't. And she didn't think it was much comfort to the Swareys either. Especially to Caleb.

She hoped he'd gotten some sleep last night. And Levi, too.

Levi. She wished she knew him better—he was such a good brother to Caleb. Such a steady presence even in his own grief. And she couldn't deny that he was handsome. His brown eyes had flicks of hazel in them, and when he looked at her, it was as if he truly saw her. Like he knew her, even though he didn't. Not really. How did he do that? And he radiated strength and kindness. She wondered what kind of sense of humor he had. Given the circumstances, she'd had no chance to see any of his humor. She imagined he could be quite light-hearted though, during normal times.

She smiled and then realized what she was doing... *Ach,* but what was wrong with her? It was Jodie's funeral today, and here she was longing after Jodie's brother. She should be ashamed of herself.

"Give me your toothbrush, Bobby," she said, a bit impatiently. "Let me put the toothpaste on it for you."

Bobby handed her his toothbrush, which was already wet and sticky with a glob of toothpaste much too big. Annie finally got them all sorted and back downstairs within ten minutes. She'd even managed to brush her own teeth.

"When will the funeral start?" she asked Thelma as they all went outside into the cold.

"Likely late-morning, and then we'll have the noon meal after the burial."

Henry was driving the buggy around to the porch to pick them up.

"There will be morning viewing before the service," Thelma went on. "I wanted to be there for that, too."

Annie nodded and helped Bobby down the steps and into the buggy. Again, she squished herself in the back seat with the children with Bobby on her lap. Henry snapped the reins and they were underway. Henry didn't have a propane heater in his buggy, and Annie could see her breath wafting out in white puffs of steam, joining the breath of the children.

Dale kept up a constant stream of chatter on the way, pointing out every single thing he saw out the window. Annie was glad for it as it lessened the heaviness of the occasion. She was almost eager to get there, as she knew the day would be full of good cheer as the people enjoyed their time together. Yet, it was still unsettling. It was one thing when it was an older person who had passed, but when it was a child... Annie shivered. She was picking up on Thelma's mood.

"You *kinner* be on your best behavior today," Henry said, glancing at them over his shoulder.

"We will, *Dat*," Debbie said.

"*I* will," George announced proudly, sticking his little chest out.

Henry pulled into the Swareys' place, and there was already a good number of buggies there. Annie thought they might be the first since it was still quite early, but she was mistaken. Henry parked their buggy in line with the others. They all got out; Thelma and Annie took the children and the food into the house while Henry tended the horse.

Annie nearly bumped into Samuel Hertz as she went into the washroom to pile all their coats on the waiting table.

"Hello, Annie."

"*Gut* morning, Samuel."

He paused while she piled the coats on top of those already there. She glanced over at him and noted his subdued expression.

"You all right?" she asked.

"I-I am, *jah*. I know dying is a part of living, but I feel bad for the Swareys. This is going to be a hard day for them."

Annie nodded, surprised by his words. Maybe this was what Marlene saw in him—this kindness and sensitivity. "You're right," she agreed softly.

"I can't imagine if I lost one of my sisters like this. But all is in *Gott's* will."

She didn't immediately respond, so he went on.

"It's hard, though, *ain't so?* Trusting, sometimes."

Her eyes widened. Hadn't she just been thinking that the day before? Maybe Samuel was more of a kindred spirit than she had thought. "*Jah,* it is," she said. "But that's hardly something a person can talk about freely..."

He gave her a rueful smile. "You're right at that," he said. "So, don't tell."

"Never," she said, more lightly. Then she smiled.

"I'm hoping Marlene makes it today. I know she'll want to be here."

"I hope so, too. Is anyone in her family here yet?"

"*Nee*. I don't think so."

"She's likely coming with them."

Someone came into the washroom with her arms full of coats and scarves.

"Hello, Barbara," Samuel said.

"*Gut* morning, Samuel," the woman replied, giving Annie the once over.

"Uh, this here is Annie Hershberger. She's the niece of Henry and Thelma."

Barbara's expression warmed. "Well, ain't that nice that you're here. Welcome, Annie."

"Thank you," Annie murmured. She gave Samuel a parting smile and left the room. Her gaze quickly found Levi who was standing near the front door now, greeting the people. He must have felt her presence, for he looked up right then and found her eyes.

She nodded slightly, and he smiled at her. She felt her pulse quicken and her cheeks grew warm. She looked away and saw Thelma, and walked over to her. Jodie's casket was still open, and people were milling about, talking. As Annie had anticipated, the mood lighter than the day before with more animated talking and laughing.

Annie spotted Jodie's mother who was sitting beside the casket. At least, she looked a bit more rested that day; although, she still had shadows beneath her eyes. Where was Caleb? Annie looked about the room but didn't see him.

And then Marlene walked in. She was moving slowly, and she had a look of concentration on her face, as if she were making every effort to be there. When she saw Annie, she broke into a smile.

Annie went over to her. "*Ach,* Marlene. I'm so happy to see you here."

Marlene swallowed, but kept her smile intact. "Can we find a place to sit?"

There were benches running along all the walls, but all the rest of the room's furniture had been removed. There was still some space on the end of one of the benches. Annie guided Marlene there, and they sat down.

"How are you doing?" Annie asked quietly.

"I-I'm here," Marlene said, her smile faltering. "Have you seen Samuel?"

"I have. I spoke with him. He's worried about you."

"*Ach,* he's always worried about me," she said, but she sounded pleased.

"That's what beaus do, *ain't so?*" Annie asked. Except in her case. How worried had Matthew been about her? She drew in a breath. But then, he hadn't really been her beau, had he? He'd been Doris's beau all along.

"Annie?"

Annie gave a start and then focused back on Marlene. "Are you staying for the burial service and the meal afterward?"

Marlene shrugged. "If I make it that long. I'm going to try."

"If you need a ride home, I'm sure *Onkel* Henry would let me use the buggy."

"Thanks, Annie. But I'm going to try to make it. I'll likely stay here instead of going to the cemetery. But there will be others who stay back, too."

"I can stay with you," Annie offered and then regretted her words. She wanted to go to the cemetery. She wanted to be there for Levi and Caleb, even though they probably wouldn't even notice her.

"*Nee.* It's not necessary, but it's nice of you to offer."

Just then, they were interrupted by little Bobby who came

over to wrap his arms around Annie's legs. She laughed and picked him up, settling him on her lap.

"Bobby, you know Marlene, don't you?"

Bobby stuck two fingers in his mouth and began sucking vigorously. Annie laughed and cuddled him close to her chest.

Chapter Eleven

The funeral service went on for over an hour. Annie couldn't take her eyes off the open casket. Neither could anyone else. She noticed everyone was fixated on the lovely young girl. Annie helped keep her little cousins quiet, though, they were surprisingly calm. When it came time for the four men to carry the casket to the waiting wagon, Annie was glad to get up and move. Thelma decided to stay back with the children, so Annie went to the graveside with Henry.

It was bitterly cold as the casket was lowered into the hand-dug hole—Annie could only imagine the labor of love involved in the digging during such weather—the hard, cold earth must have made it nearly impossible. Mr. and Mrs. Swarey were the first to toss a handful of soil on top of the casket. Annie couldn't help herself. She winced when she heard the frozen dirt clods hit the casket. And then Levi threw in a handful of dirt. Caleb, who hadn't left Levi's side during the funeral, held his dirt tightly in his hand. Everyone was waiting for him to throw it into the grave, but he didn't seem able to do it. Levi looked down at him, his expression urging him to toss the dirt.

But Caleb couldn't do it. Finally, Levi pried the dirt from his brother's hand and dropped it into the grave for him. Mrs. Swarey moved close and put her arm around Caleb. Caleb was weeping silently.

And then after a final prayer, it was over. Everyone headed back to their buggies and to the Swarey farm. Those who had stayed behind would have the meal ready. Annie and Henry were both silent on the way back. Once they arrived, Henry again saw to the horse while Annie went ahead inside. The house was now filled with a sense of relief. It was almost palpable to Annie. She, too, felt more relaxed.

Marlene introduced her to many of the Hollybrook people, and she began to feel a bit more like part of the community. She stuck to Marlene's side as much as she could, but she also wanted to be helpful to the Swareys. After about an hour, she realized that every time she got up to take dishes into the kitchen or to see to one of the children, Levi was somewhere close beside her. He didn't always speak to her, he just seemed to be always *there*.

Once she realized it, it gave her a sense of peace. She only prayed that her presence was comforting to him, too.

When it was time to go, she bid Marlene a fond farewell, promising to visit soon. Then she helped Thelma get all the children into the buggy. As they were pulling away, she glanced out the window. Levi had come out to the porch and was watching her. She raised her hand slightly and he raised his in response.

The look of sadness in his eyes haunted her.

Levi was relieved when the last buggy left that day. It had been a good funeral, as those things went, but he was exhausted. It wasn't their way to show grief in public—more than a tear or two. His parents had held up well, but he knew they were ready to drop. And Caleb? He had disappeared right after the burial service. Levi was almost certain he was hiding out in the barn again, and he didn't blame him.

The guilt that ate away at Caleb was also eating at him. If only he'd locked the gun away. He knew his parents didn't hold him accountable. In their minds, it had been entirely on Caleb. They had forgiven his little brother, or they would forgive him—for that was their way. But it would take some time, maybe a lot of time, before things would ever be normal again.

Normal? Who was he kidding? Things would never be the way they had been. Normal was going to be something completely different from now on.

Ah, Jodie, I miss you, little sister. He sighed heavily and leaned back against the headboard of his bed. He closed his eyes and felt tears burn the back of his eyes. Tomorrow would be better, he thought. Every day would get better, wouldn't it? Wasn't that how things went. Time heals all wounds, folks were fond of saying. Right then, he wished time would speed up.

Yet, he didn't. Would his memories of Jodie fade with time? Would they dissipate into the air? Right then, he wished that having photographs wasn't forbidden. He wanted pictures of Jodie. Pictures of her laughing and running across the yard and playing with their goats. He wanted pictures of the twinkle in her eye when he teased her, the way her lips curled into the brightest of smiles when *Mamm* made cinnamon rolls. Even just one picture. One photo to cherish and bring out to look at on occasion.

In his mind's eye, he saw Jodie again, lying in her casket. She'd never been that still in life. Maybe when she slept. But never otherwise. *Dat* used to laugh all the time about how the grass never grew under Jodie's feet.

Jodie. Jodie. Jodie.

He heard something then. He listened intently. There it was again. He got up and went to his door to listen. Sobbing. That was what it was. He cracked his door open to hear better. It was his mother. She was in her room, crying. He squeezed his eyes shut, every sob of his mother cutting through him.

Why hadn't he locked the gun away? Why had there been rats in the barn? Why had Caleb wanted to be the hero?

Why wasn't Jodie tucked away in her bed, sleeping soundly?

Why?

Levi shut his door and went back to bed. His mind wouldn't stop circling the funeral. Scenes from the day unfolded before him. That Annie Hershberger was a nice girl. In some strange way, she had comforted him just by being there. What was it about her? She had a steadiness, a warmth that settled around her.

He hoped he'd see her again soon. He could use some steadiness in his life right now. And some warmth.

He drew the quilt over his shoulders and did his best to turn his mind off.

Chapter Twelve

Annie was frustrated. It took her forever to type out the simplest words on the computer. Goodness, but why weren't the letters in alphabetical order? That would be a whole lot easier. There seemed to be no rhyme nor reason for their placement on the keyboard.

And why call it a keyboard? In her mind, a keyboard would be someplace to hang keys. And a screen? A screen was something to keep mosquitoes and flies out of the kitchen.

Despite her frustration, she had to laugh. Learning to work on a computer required learning a whole new language. She was worried her uncle was going to be aggravated with her because she was taking so long to do the simplest things on it. But he wasn't.

"How's it coming?" he asked, popping into the office.

She blew out her breath. "I've only put in two customers," she said, feeling like a one-year-old learning to feed herself. "I'm sorry. It's taking me forever."

Henry laughed. "You'll get better at it. It took me a right long time to get the hang of it myself."

"By the end of the day, I'll have done a whole five minutes of work," she said.

He laughed again. "It can't be that bad."

"Oh *jah,* it can."

He circled her desk to lean over her. "See, you're making progress."

"Truth be told, *Onkel*, you had to be hoping for better than this."

"Don't you go putting words in my mouth. It takes a lot of learning."

"How do the *Englisch* do it? How do they put in words quickly?"

"They have a certain way of holding their hands over the keyboard. That's what I was told, anyway. I never got the knack of it."

"I don't think I ever will either."

"You'll find your way. Are you ready for some lunch?"

"It can't be lunch time already!"

"But it is."

"You go on ahead. I'm going to stay here until I at least get four people entered." She laughed, but she wasn't feeling very amused.

"All right. I'll have Thelma fix you up something and bring it back to you. Shall I leave the store open, then? Can you take care of anyone who comes in?"

"*Jah*. I can. Don't fret. I'll be fine."

"All right, Annie. I'll be back in an hour."

"Take your time," she told him, hoping she really could handle any forthcoming customers. She knew how to ring up purchases on the old cash register, but she wasn't too confident of the credit card machine. Henry had showed her how to use it a couple times, but still, she was unsure of herself.

With luck, no one would come in. She gave a soft snort. What was she doing? Wishing for no customers? What kind of employee was she? She shook her head. She most certainly had a ways to go before she was going to be of any real help to her aunt and uncle. Maybe she should stay home with the children and let Thelma come in and work.

She bent over the keyboard, searching for the "p". She

touched it and watched the letter appear on the screen. It was magic, really, the way the computer worked.

She heard the front door close, thinking it was Henry leaving. But then she heard someone calling out, "Hello? Anyone here?"

She jumped up and hurried out to the floor. Samuel was there, his hat in his hand.

"Oh, hello, Samuel," she said. "I'm afraid you just missed my *onkel*."

"In truth, I was looking for you."

She blanched. "Why?"

He walked over to her and smiled. "I was wondering if you'd seen Marlene today."

"*Nee*. I saw her yesterday, the same as you."

"How did she seem to you? Better?"

Annie frowned. "Not really. But she was there, and that's something, isn't it?"

"*Jah*." He fingered the rim of his hat. "It's hard for her, and I don't know how to help her."

"I don't think we can help her. We can pray..."

"She takes medicine sometimes which helps. But she won't take it all the time. She says the expense puts too much burden on her family."

"But doesn't the district have an emergency fund for such things?"

He nodded. "She doesn't want her family to drain it."

"But the whole reason..." Annie sighed, and a wave of sorrow washed over her at the thought of Marlene's suffering.

"I know, I know. I've tried talking her into taking the medicines more regularly. The herbs Old Mae gives her help a bit, but not enough."

"I'm so sorry."

"I thought maybe you'd have an idea on how to help."

Her? How could she have an idea? Besides, Annie felt a bit uncomfortable discussing Marlene like this. It seemed like a betrayal, although, Annie couldn't think why that would be.

"*Nee*," she said, "*nee*, I don't have any ideas."

Samuel had taken one step closer. "I wish Marlene was healthy like you, Annie."

Annie stepped back.

Samuel must have seen the look of surprise on her face, for he quickly said, "I'm sorry. That was a silly thing to say. I meant... Well, I meant..." He blew out his breath is a gush. "I just wish Marlene didn't hurt so much."

Annie wished he would leave. She was totally uncomfortable now. "I, uh, I have work to do."

"Of course," he said. "I'll see you around, Annie."

Before she could respond, he left the store. She stood there for a moment, trying to figure out what had just happened. Finally, she shook her head and sighed. She hoped Samuel wouldn't come in again for a very long time.

Chapter Thirteen

"I want to leave," Caleb said, sniffing and wiping his nose.

"What do you mean?" Levi said, sitting down on Caleb's bed.

Caleb paced the room and then stopped, putting his hands on his hips. "I want to go away. I shouldn't be here. *Mamm* and *Dat* hate me, and I don't blame them."

"They don't hate you."

"*Jah,* they do. I... k-killed Jodie." Caleb raised his chin as if defying himself not to cry.

"It was an accident," Levi said. "We all know that. And I'm just as much to blame. I should have locked the gun away. I'm so sorry about that, Caleb. Truly, truly sorry."

Caleb stared at him. "It ain't your fault. I was the one who took the gun. I was the one ... who ... pulled the trigger." His voice caught, but his eyes remained dry as he stared at Levi.

"Caleb, it was an accident. It's over. There ain't a thing we can do to bring Jodie back." Levi worked to keep his voice steady.

"I want her ... back," Caleb said, and his resolve not to cry crumbled. Tears coursed down his cheeks. "I want her back."

"We all do," Levi said. "All of us. But it can't happen. Jodie is in heaven now."

"*Gott* don't need her up there. We need her down here."

Levi patted the quilt next to him. "Sit down, Caleb. Please."

Caleb sat down and leaned against Levi.

"We can't question the ways of *Gott*. We just have to trust him." Even as he said the words, Levi knew that he questioned the ways of God. More and more of late, but he didn't want to admit that to Caleb. Or perhaps, he didn't want to admit it to himself.

"I-I trust *Gott*," Caleb said, but his voice faltered, and Levi knew Caleb was trying to say the right thing, just as he was.

"Get into bed, now," Levi said gently. "You'll feel better tomorrow, and the day after that. And don't ever doubt the love of *Mamm* and *Dat*, or me, either. We all love you, Caleb. It was an accident. All right?"

Caleb nodded against him, and Levi stood and put him to

bed. He squeezed Caleb's shoulder. "*Gut*-night, Caleb. I'll see you tomorrow. It'll be better. Every day, it will. I promise."

"Night," Caleb mumbled.

Levi stood for a moment, looking down at his brother. Then he picked up the lantern and left the room.

Chapter Fourteen

Annie had a letter. When she recognized the writing as her mother's, she was excited. Although she hadn't been gone but a couple of weeks, Annie missed her family. She especially missed Betty. She usually spent a lot of time with her little sister, and it was odd not to see her regularly. Not that Annie didn't enjoy her cousins at Thelma's and Henry's house, but sleeping out in the *daadi haus*, she got lonely. In truth, she wasn't sure why she even lived in the *daadi haus*, as she spent almost all her time at the big house.

"You gonna open it now?" Debbie asked her.

"I think I'll wait and open it at the *daadi haus*."

"Why?" Dale asked her. He reached out as if to take the letter from her.

Debbie slapped his hand. "You can't take her letter," she scolded. "It's hers."

Dale sent up a wail. "You hit me! *Mamm*, Debbie's hittin' me!"

"That's enough," Annie interrupted. "Debbie, you apologize to your brother. You know we don't hit each other."

"Sorry," Debbie said grumpily.

Dale scrubbed at his tears with his fist.

"How come I don't get no letters?" George asked.

"Cause you don't got anybody to write to you," Debbie said.

Annie stuck her letter in her waistband. "Let's go see what Bobby is up to, shall we?" she asked, hoping to distract them. "I'm sure he wants someone to play with."

"Bobby could write me a letter," George said.

"Bobby can't even write his own name yet," Dale said.

George scowled.

"I'll write you a letter," Dale told him, taking his hand. "How's that?"

George's face brightened. "I can write you one, too."

"You can't write your name, neither," Debbie observed.

"All right, *kinner*, how about I get some paper and we'll all write letters to each other. How does that sound?" Annie's suggestion was well received, and all of them went straight to the front room to dig out a tablet of paper from the bureau. Annie fetched the tin of crayons and a couple pencils and set them all up at the dining room table. Bobby found them and crawled up on the bench, too. Within minutes, they were all happily writing or scribbling across pieces of paper.

Annie looked up to see Thelma grinning at her from the kitchen doorway.

Levi brushed Clipper down and gave her a handful of sugar cubes. "There you go, girl," he said as Clipper snuffed the sugar from his hand. "You're a *gut* horse, you know that."

Clipper nuzzled Levi's arm and then shook her mane. Levi smiled and left the stall, closing the door behind him. He put the brush on the shelf that ran along the front left wall of the barn. Then he glanced down to where the family's bike always rested. It was gone. That was curious. There'd been ice on the ground that morning. He couldn't imagine anyone taking the bike out in that.

Maybe his dad was working on it. The long winter months were a good time to be checking over all their equipment, and the bicycle fell into that category. He looked around the barn but didn't see it anywhere. He knew for sure and for certain that his mother wouldn't have taken the bike out, and it was unlikely that his dad would be riding it around either. Which left only one other person.

Caleb.

Levi moaned. Caleb had been acting strangely lately, which was to be expected, Levi supposed. Some days he would talk and other days, he would keep strictly to himself. Some days he joined the family for meals and other days, he found one excuse or another to either skip them or eat later by himself. *Mamm* and *Dat* had given him a wide margin, understanding that he was hurting. So had Levi.

But now, Levi wondered. Had Caleb taken the bike out in this weather? And if so, where had he gone? Maybe, he was visiting Jodie's gravesite. That would make sense. Levi went to the barn door and studied the sky. It looked like it could snow again at any minute. The last big snow had mostly melted off, but the temperatures still hovered around freezing. If the skies started dumping snow, then Caleb might have a hard time making it back home.

Levi decided to hitch up the pony cart and go to the cemetery himself. First, he ran to the house to tell his mother he'd be back soon.

"Is Caleb with you? And where are you going?" she called after him.

"An errand," he said vaguely and then made his way back to the barn. He didn't mention that Caleb wasn't out there with him. He didn't want to worry her. Besides, he could be at the cemetery within thirty minutes, and he could throw the bicycle into the back of the cart and give Caleb a ride home.

He took Clipper out of her stall. "Sorry, girl," he said. "I just got you all settled, but this shouldn't take too long."

Clipper didn't protest being hitched up.

"When we get back, I'll give you some more sugar, how's that?" Levi asked, petting her nose. "But in the meantime, let's go find Caleb."

They started out of the yard and onto the road. The *Englisch* kept the roads well plowed during the winter for which their district was mighty grateful. The *Englisch* even plowed well onto the shoulder of the roads, where hundreds of Amish buggies had formed grooves in the asphalt. In any case, most of the snow was gone, and there were only occasional chunks of ice and dirty snow along the way. Clipper wasn't bothered by it, and she clip-clopped steadily on.

Levi turned down the road where the Amish cemetery was located. He saw the rows of modest headstones ahead of him. He scanned the flat expanse, his eyes settling on the fresh mound of dirt where his sister's body lay. Caleb wasn't there. He pulled up on the reins, secured them, and jumped out of the cart. He strode across the frozen grass, crunching his way to Jodie's grave. There were no bicycle treads obvious. Caleb hadn't been there.

Levi paused, staring down at the grave, his heart heavy. He'd told Caleb that every day would get better, but so far, his grief hadn't lessened. Neither had his guilt.

"I'm sorry," he whispered to the air. "I'm sorry."

He took a deep breath, feeling the icy air burn his lungs. He waited another moment before turning back to the pony cart. Where was Caleb, anyway? If he hadn't come here, Levi wasn't certain where he would have gone. But then, for all he knew, Caleb could already be home again. This whole trip was likely a fool's mission. Maybe *Mamm* had sent Caleb for something.

No. She'd asked if Caleb was with him, so that wouldn't make sense.

There was nothing for it, but to return home. Levi climbed into the buggy and snapped the reins. Clipper kept up a good pace on the way back home. Levi drove the cart straight to the barn. Before unhitching the horse, he ran inside the barn looking for the bike.

Still gone.

Sighing, he went back to take care of Clipper, giving her the promised additional sugar treats. Then he walked back to the house. He thought maybe Caleb had leaned the bike against the front porch, but it wasn't there either.

He found his mother in the kitchen. "*Mamm,* have you seen Caleb?"

She turned. "*Nee.*" Her forehead creased. "I thought he was with you."

"*Nee.*"

She tossed down the dishtowel and rushed past Levi. "Caleb!" she called. "Caleb!" She hurried to the bottom of the stairs. "Are you up there?"

No response.

She stepped to the front room. "Walter, you see Caleb recently?"

Walter looked up from his book. "*Nee.*" He peered around his wife. "Levi? Ain't Caleb with you?"

Levi swallowed. "The bicycle is gone."

Walter shot up out of his chair. "*What?*"

Leah clasped her chest. "*Ach, nee*. Walter, where is he?"

"I went to the cemetery," Levi said, and they both stared at him. "I thought maybe he was there, but he wasn't."

"You knew the bike was gone and you never told us?" his father asked, his voice raising in pitch.

"I thought I knew where he was," Levi said. "I'm sorry. I went to fetch him."

"It's cold out there," Leah said. She put her hand on Walter's arm. "Walter, it's too cold to be riding a bicycle."

Walter let out his breath. "I know. Don't fret. He's likely gone to a friend's house."

"What friend? Lately, he won't be talking to anyone." Leah looked at Levi. "Has he talked to you? He won't talk to me or your father."

"He's hurting," Levi said. "He thinks we all hate him."

"*Hate* him?" Walter said. "It was an accident. We all *know* that."

"But he doesn't," Levi said. "Not in his heart. He blames himself." *Like I blame myself,* he thought, but didn't say.

"We have to go," Leah said, her voice frantic. "We have to find him."

"*Nee.* You must stay here," Walter said. "Levi and I will go. You have to stay here so someone will be home when he comes back."

"But he's run away," Leah said, her voice cracking.

"We don't *know* that," Walter told her. "You stay here. Levi? Come on. Let's go."

Levi hadn't yet taken off his coat or scarf, so he was ready. It only took his father a few seconds to bundle up, and they were out of the house, hurrying to the barn. Poor Clipper likely didn't know what to think when she was hitched up for the third time.

Chapter Fifteen

Caleb was cold. So cold, he felt it eat into his bones. But he couldn't stop. He had to keep riding. He had to get so far away that no one would ever find him. The only thing he knew to do was to keep to the road that led out of town. Occasional cars zipped by him, creating such a gush of wind that it nearly knocked him off the bike more than once. But he lowered his head and forged on.

His fingers had frozen to the handlebars. He was sure of it, for he could no longer feel them. The gloves he'd put on were worthless against the frigid air. His legs were freezing, too, but he kept moving them. Round and round and round. He blinked; his eyes dry from the air. Glancing up, he wondered if it was going to start snowing. If it did, he'd have real trouble staying upright through it.

Where was he to go? He had no idea. He hadn't thought this out—he just couldn't bear it for another minute at home. He couldn't bear walking by Jodie's empty room. He couldn't bear her empty place at the table. He couldn't bear the *silence* of it all. *Ach,* how her constant chattering used to get on his last nerve.

Now, he would give his life to hear her once again.

No. Don't think about it. Just pedal. Just pedal. Keep going. He'd find someplace to hole up. There had to be a barn somewhere, where he could hide and spend the night. Then, the next morning, he'd hit it again. Maybe he could pedal all the way to Indianapolis. He wasn't sure how far that was, but he could get lost in the people there. He'd heard the city was huge. Surely, he could disappear.

Disappear and never be found again.

His *mamm* and *dat* would be sad at first. Maybe even worried. But they'd be better off without him. Better off without the constant reminder of what he'd done. In fact, Hollybrook would be better off without him. He couldn't face anyone. Couldn't bear to see the pity in their eyes. And the accusation. At the funeral, so many folks went out of their way to pat his back and murmur their condolences. But he knew the truth. He knew what they were really thinking.

That he killed his sister.

They were grateful that he wasn't *their* son—that he wasn't part of their families. They hadn't said as much, but he saw it in their eyes. Every look hammered through him to his already broken heart. He couldn't take it.

He didn't want to see anyone from Hollybrook ever again.

He sucked in a breath and felt it burn into his lungs. Dear Lord, it was cold out here. He'd find shelter soon. Or maybe he shouldn't look for shelter, maybe he should just keep going until he froze to the bicycle. He would eventually fall over into the ditch. A frozen boy.

He would die. Of course, he would die, but would that be so bad? He'd get to see Jodie again. Wait. Would she speak to him in heaven? Maybe she hated him, too. Maybe she wouldn't have a thing to do with him. Even in heaven, he'd be alone.

Ach. He wouldn't be in heaven. What was he thinking? God would never let him in, not after what he'd done.

His eyes burned with tears that dried as fast as they formed. The air hurt. His eyes hurt. Could a person go blind in the cold? His legs were slowing down now. His speed had dropped to barely faster than a walk. *Keep pedaling,* he ordered himself. *Keep going.*

He spotted a farm up ahead. It was an Amish farm, for there were no electrical wires, and he spotted a buggy around the side of the barn. He had no idea who lived there. He had to be quite far from Hollybrook by then. His chest hurt as if someone were sitting on him. He struggled to grab a breath. He'd sneak into the barn. He wasn't ready to die yet. Jodie wouldn't want him. God, for sure, wouldn't want him.

His legs barely worked to get to the barn. He peeled his hands from the handlebars and stiffly got off the bike, nearly losing his balance. He forced himself around the back of the barn where he leaned his bike against the rough wooden wall. He hoped no one was watching him. He was too stiff, too cold, to sneak around the barn. He needed to stay low, but he could hardly move as it was.

Somehow, he made his way around to the door and managed to get it open. He closed it again and heard animals stir. A cow bellowed.

"H-hush," he stammered. "Shh."

There was barely any light inside the barn. He stood a minute, ready to drop, waiting for his eyes to adjust to the darkness. He let out a shaky breath and realized he was trembling so hard he was ready to collapse.

Not yet, he told himself. *Not yet.*

He found a horse blanket that had been dropped on a bench. His hands, claw-like now, worked to pick it up. Quivering, he managed to wrap it around himself. Then he saw a pile of hay in the corner. He stumbled to it, burrowed himself inside, tugging the blanket closer around him. It was a relief to be out of the wind. He felt blood begin to surge and tingle back into his limbs. He closed his eyes.

He was tired. So very, very tired. Tomorrow, he would think of what to do next. Or today. Was it nighttime? He was confused. He couldn't think straight. He gave up, falling asleep instantly.

Before supper had been served and cleared away, Annie went back to the *daadi haus*. By that time, her letter was burning under her waistband, wanting to be read. She chuckled at the thought, but hurried nevertheless to light a lantern, and stir up the fire in the warming stove. She pulled a rocker close to the stove and pulled out the envelope. She opened it quickly, pressing the letter flat on her lap.

Dearest Annie,

How are you, daughter? I know you're fine and likely being a big help to your aenti and onkel. How are the kinner? I reckon they're right glad to have you around. We're missing you around here. Betty misses you the most. Thank you for writing her the other day. She treasures that letter, and I dare say, it's in tatters from being read so many times.

All your brothers are fine, as are we all. Give my greetings to Thelma and the family, will you? I suppose I should be writing Thelma, too, and I'll find the time sometime this week.

There's something I want to tell you before you hear it somewhere else. It's about Matthew and Doris...

Annie stiffened. She looked away from the letter and took a deep breath before continuing.

...They're getting married in a week. I know it's right fast—there has been a lot of talk. But Matthew was overheard saying that he's waited a long time for Doris, and he's not of a mind to wait any longer. The bishop has put his blessing on it, so it's happening. I want to put your mind at rest, though. No one knows of your short engagement to Matthew.

Short engagement? That was for sure and for certain. *Ach*, it had been less than twenty-four hours. Annie pressed her lips together and shook her head. Twenty-four hours was plenty of time to get excited. Plenty of time to dream about a future that was never going to happen. Plenty of time to get your heart broken.

I regret saying this, daughter, but your dat feels that you should come home for the wedding. Linder Creek ain't that far from Hollybrook, so it wouldn't take you long to get here. Betty would be over the moon to have you home for a spell. And you wouldn't have to stay too long.

Your dat seems quite insistent on it. I tried to reason with him, but he ain't budging.

I'm sure Thelma and Henry won't mind if you leave for a couple of days. The wedding is next Tuesday. If you're home on Monday, that should suit. You can take the bus back again on Wednesday.

I'm thinking of you, daughter, and am right excited myself to see you again.

Much love,

Mamm

Annie clasped her hands on top of the letter. Go back to Linder Creek? Be forced to sit through her former beau's wedding? Have to hear Matthew and Doris make promises to each other? What was her father thinking? Was he trying to torture her? She stood up and the letter fluttered to the floor. She walked to the window and peered out into the darkness.

She didn't want to go. She could pretend she never got the letter. She could simply not show up. The window glass was cold as she pressed her face against it. No. She couldn't lie. She would have to go.

She closed her eyes. The smell of the warming stove filled the air, and she breathed in the woody scent. She would be all right. Of course, she could.

Wasn't she over Matthew by now?

She stilled and searched her heart. The hurt had lessened. It wasn't nearly as acute as it had been directly after Matthew had called off their engagement. In truth, she wondered if she was only nursing hurt feelings now, not really the loss of his love.

And then, someone else's face crowded into her mind, shoving Matthew's image aside.

Levi Swarey.

Her heart squeezed. How was he that evening? Was he still reeling from his sister's death? Was he still feeling guilty? Was he sleeping at night—or did he toss and turn with the weight of it all?

She backed away from the window and turned to see her mother's letter lying on the floor. She had no idea why her father was insisting on her attendance. It made no sense—not really. But she would go. She would hold her head high and go.

And then she realized what day it was and what date she'd seen on her mother's letter. Why, the wedding was happening *almost immediately*. Her mother's letter must have somehow gotten delayed. Annie didn't even have time to write her back—she barely had time to get her bus ticket.

She should be panicked, but she wasn't. When she bent down to pick up the letter to recheck the date, her mind was even not on Matthew's and Doris's upcoming wedding.

Instead, her thoughts were firmly on Levi Swarey.

Chapter Sixteen

"We'll head to Jason's house," Walter said, snapping the reins.

"*Gut* idea. Hopefully, he'll be there." But even as Levi said the words, he knew his brother wouldn't be there, visiting his friend. Caleb had run away. Levi hadn't said so, but he was certain of it. So, where would Caleb have gone? And on a bicycle? When had he left? Hopefully, he hadn't gotten far. But where would he be in this cold? He could die of exposure.

Was that what Caleb wanted? To die like Jodie had died? He shuddered. No. Surely not. But fear crept through him just the same.

"Hurry, *Dat*. It's getting colder by the minute."

His father's face was set in a grim expression. Levi could see it even in the shadows. The headlights on their buggy bounced over the road as Clipper kept up a good pace. Levi stared out the window, trying to make out something, anything, any shape, that could be his brother. *Ach,* but it was impossible. They'd never find him in the dark.

They reached Jason's home and turned into the drive. "I'll check," Levi said, jumping out of the buggy. He took the steps two at a time and knocked on the door. Jason's father answered.

"Why, Levi Swarey, what brings you out tonight?"

"Is Caleb here?" Levi said, without preamble.

Thomas frowned. "*Nee.* He ain't. What's going on?"

"He's gone missing." Levi took a breath. No reason to alarm the whole district. At least, not yet. "I mean, he hasn't come home yet." He forced a chuckle. "Probably arrived right after *Dat* and I left. Anyway, just checking around a bit."

Thomas's brow creased. "I can help you look—"

"Thank you," Levi said. "Like I said, he may have returned by now. How about I come by later if he hasn't. We'd be glad for the help then."

Thomas nodded. "All right. I'll wait for word." He glanced out to the yard. "It's getting wicked cold out. I would hate to think..."

"I know. I'll be back if need be." Levi turned and hurried back down the steps. He got into the buggy. "He ain't there. Thomas has offered to help look."

"We may need him," Walter said, his voice suddenly sounding very old. "I don't rightly know where to look next."

"He may have tried to ride out of town," Levi said. "We can take the road toward Indianapolis."

He glanced over at his father and saw his shoulders shaking. Was he crying? Levi swallowed hard. Oh, dear Lord, it was too much. Caleb running off on the tail of the crisis with Jodie. He reached over and put his hand on his father's arm.

"It'll be all right, *Dat*. We'll find him. You'll see." Levi send up a frantic prayer.

Walter sniffed and swiped at his tears with his gloved hand. "I know, son. *Gott* is with us, and He's with Caleb, too."

"*Jah*," Levi murmured. He shifted his attention back out the window. The beam of light from the headlamps hardly stretched to the side of the road. He didn't say it out loud, but they'd need a complete miracle to find Caleb like this. He was hardly going to be standing on the side of the road in the buggy grooves. He had run away. He was hiding somewhere.

Somewhere in the dark where they would never find him.

They rode on in silence for another thirty minutes. Levi knew they weren't covering many miles, but then, Caleb likely wouldn't have either. Still, with every rotation of the wheels,

Levi's anguish deepened. Where was Caleb? Had he found shelter? If Levi wasn't so sorry for the state of his brother's heart and mind, he'd be angry at him for causing such anguish.

Finally, his father pulled up on the reins. "We're heading back. Hopefully, he went home."

"If he didn't, Thomas will help us look. Others will too, if they know."

Walter shook his head. "It ain't doing us any *gut* in the dark. Come morning, I'll spread the word." He cleared his throat. "If he's not already home, that is."

"All right." Levi sank back. His father was right. Driving around in the dark was doing them no good. He wondered how his mother was faring. And then, suddenly, his thoughts went to Annie Hershberger. He felt an odd urge to tell her Caleb was missing. She'd been so kind to him—to both of them. He wished she knew what was happening. She would pray. Maybe, she would even have an idea of where to look for Caleb.

No. That was silly. Of course, she wouldn't have an idea. She hardly knew the area. Hardly knew Caleb, for that matter. Still, he wished she knew. He wished he could look into her eyes and see her faith and her strength.

He wished he could have met Annie under different conditions. He likely would have asked to court her. But how could he even think of such a thing now? With all the heartache in his family? And besides, he had played a huge part in Jodie's death. How could he be thinking of something so selfish as courting Annie when he had so much to answer for?

For the hundredth time, he asked himself why he hadn't locked the gun away.

For the hundredth time, he felt the guilt twist through him.

"Levi?"

Levi gave a start and glanced over at his father. "*Jah?*"

"It wasn't anybody's fault," he said. "It was an accident."

"I keep telling Caleb that."

"I wasn't talking about Caleb."

Levi sucked in his breath.

Walter put his hand on Levi's knee. "I know you're blaming yourself. I could just as easily be blaming myself. It was my gun."

"But I used it last."

"I know you did, son. But we don't always lock it away. I thought putting it up that high was safety enough. I was wrong. So, I could be carrying heavy guilt, too."

"But *Dat*, it was me who used it last."

"Levi," Walter said, his voice stern but not unkind, "we can argue all we want about who's guilty. Jodie is gone. Nothing will bring her back. You're telling Caleb it was an accident. Maybe, you should start telling yourself."

Levi's throat swelled around the growing lump of tears. How did his dad know how guilty he felt? He thought he'd been hiding it well enough.

"All right, *Dat*," he mumbled. But could he? Could he put his guilt down?

He had no idea.

"Try," Walter said, as if reading his mind. "Try. Give it to *Gott*. He loves all of us, even though we might doubt it."

Levi's eyes filled with tears. He nodded, not trusting himself to speak. Walter sighed and took his hand from Levi's knee, snapping the reins over Clipper.

"C'mon, girl," his dad called out to the horse. "Let's get you home. And hopefully, Caleb is back."

Caleb wasn't back. When Levi and his father entered the house, Leah rushed at them, hope stamped on her face. When she saw that they were alone, she crumpled against Walter, weeping.

"You-you didn't find him," she cried.

"It was too dark to see anything," Walter said, putting his arms around her and leading her to the davenport. He sat down with her. "We'll look in the morning, and Thomas is going to help us."

"Jason's *dat*? So, Caleb wasn't there."

"*Nee*," Walter said gently. "But Caleb has a *gut* head on his shoulders. He'll have found someplace safe to pass the night."

"Can I get you some tea, *Mamm*?" Levi asked, feeling helpless standing there.

She looked up at him with teary eyes and shook her head. "*Nee. Nee*. I-I don't want anything."

"*Dat's* right," Levi said. "Caleb is smart. He's tucked away somewhere safe. We'll find him come morning."

She nodded but didn't look in the least convinced. She looked at Walter. "So, we just wait out the night?"

Walter nodded. "It's all we can do."

"Should we call the police?" she asked. "The *Englischers* might know what to do."

"They can't do any more than we can in the dark." Walter sighed. "If we don't find Caleb in the morning, I'll call them. I promise."

Levi's eyes widened slightly at that. For his father to even consider calling the *Englisch* only showed how upset he truly was. "*Dat*? Can I get you anything?"

"*Nee.* Go on up to bed. Your mother and I will be up shortly."

Levi gave him a questioning look.

"Go on," his father repeated.

Levi took one of the lit lanterns and left, climbing the stairs slowly. In the hallway, he paused outside of Caleb's room. Then he glanced across the hall to Jodie's empty room. Both of his siblings were gone. Both of them. The upstairs nearly wept with emptiness. Levi forced himself to keep breathing. Forced himself to be reasonable. Caleb would be found. By tomorrow night, he'd be all snug in his bed.

"Please, *Gott,* let it be so," he muttered as he made his way to his room.

Chapter Seventeen

After reading her mother's letter, Annie went back to the big house. She wanted to help Thelma fix supper. Perhaps, she'd even beat Thelma to it and could have some of it ready by the time her aunt realized what time it was. That would be even better.

She let herself in the side door and walked quietly into the kitchen. She fumbled around a bit in the growing darkness until she located the lantern and the matches. The room sprang to life. She saw that Thelma had set out the dishes for the meal, and since nothing was cooking, it appeared that left-overs were on the menu. With smooth movements, Annie set about getting things ready, knowing by then where everything was. She was just ready to heat up the griddle to warm up slices of meatloaf when Thelma came in, yawning.

"*Ach,* I thought I heard you in here," she said. "The time got away from me today."

"I thought I'd get a start on things."

"You don't have to help get the meals, you know. You're hired to work in the shop."

"Are you saying you don't want my help?" Annie teased.

Thelma laughed. "Hardly. I'll take every bit of help you want to offer."

Annie hesitated and then said, "Thelma, you know I got that letter..."

"*Jah.* Was it from your *mamm*?"

"It was."

"How is everything?"

"Fine." Annie switched on the burner of the cook stove. "*Dat* wants me to come home for a few days..."

Thelma put the tea kettle down. "Oh?"

"Matthew Wanner and Doris Glick are getting married. *Dat* wants me there for the wedding. I'd only be gone three days. One day to get there, the wedding day, and then back the next day. But I'd have to leave right away. Is it all right?"

"Annie, you're not trapped here. If you need to go home, then you feel free to go."

Annie gave a rueful laugh. "I know I'm not trapped, *Aenti*. Truth be told, I don't really want to go home."

Thelma's brow rose.

"I'd just as soon miss the wedding—"

Thelma gave a small gasp, and her expression turned sympathetic. "Wait. Matthew Wanner. Doris Glick? Aren't they the cousins who aren't really cousins?"

Annie sighed. So her mother had told Thelma her story. "*Jah*."

"No wonder you don't want to go... But your *dat* wants you there?"

Annie nodded.

"Then you must go."

Sometimes Annie resisted the notion that a girl had to obey every single thing her father wanted. Usually, it didn't bother her that much, but right then, she'd like to stand up to him and tell him no.

Thelma walked over to her and put her arms around her. "I'm sorry. Will it be hard? *Ach*, what am I saying? Of course, it'll be hard."

Annie leaned against her for a moment before turning back to the cook stove. "I don't know how I'll feel. I'm not as hurt as I was. Leaving Linder Creek helped. Being here with all of you, helps. And I like my work at the shop."

Thelma smiled. "I'm glad. It's been right *gut* to have you here. And Henry tells me how much you're helping."

"I truly like working there. And I have to confess, I like learning the computer."

"Ain't it a marvel?"

Annie laughed. "That it is."

"So, we need to get you a bus ticket then."

"*Jah*. I think I'll need to buy it at the station tomorrow right before I board."

"Tomorrow? *Ach*, as soon as that? Henry can drive you to the station. Do you have money?"

"I have money."

"All right, then." Thelma went back to the kettle and filled it with water. "Let's get this meal put together. The *kinner* will be clamoring for food any minute."

Levi stood at his bedroom window, praying for daylight. He disliked these short days of winter when the sun didn't rise for hours. He knew it was futile to go looking for Caleb this early. But the moment the sun came up over the bare trees, he would be ready. He listened and thought he heard his mother already stirring in the kitchen. Had she slept at all last night?

He listened more closely and heard nothing more. He must have been mistaken.

Levi hadn't gotten more than an hour or two of sleep himself. He had spent most of the night staring up at the dark ceiling, praying for his brother's safety. Where was Caleb? Had he kept warm?

Levi sighed and turned away from the window. He could see to Clipper, make sure she was fed and watered. Levi hurriedly put on his suspenders and went downstairs.

Caleb was dreaming. He was playing with Jodie, and she was pushing him playfully as they took turns swinging. It was odd, though, because the swing didn't go up. He stayed in place, even though Jodie pushed on his back over and over again. He was getting irritated. Why wasn't the swing taking flight? What was holding him back?

"Son? Son? Wake up." The voice filtered into his sleep and Caleb stirred. "Son? Get up. C'mon now."

Caleb opened his eyes and blinked into the yellow stream of light from a flashlight. He could barely see anything as the light was so directly in his eyes.

"Huh?" he muttered.

"Get on up," said the low voice. "What are you doing out here? It's a wonder you didn't freeze to death."

"Huh?" Caleb said again, trying to put together the pieces. And then he remembered. He'd run away. He'd hidden in someone's barn. *This* someone, who was now shining a light in his face. Caleb jumped up so fast, he nearly fell over. He was cold. His limbs were stiff.

"What are you doing out here?" the voice asked again.

"I-I needed someplace to sleep." Caleb's voice wasn't working very well. Goodness, but he was cold. He started to shiver.

"You in trouble?" the man asked.

"I-I..." Caleb drew in a shaky breath. "*Nee.* I'm not in trouble."

"Your folks know you're gone?"

"By now, they do."

"Come on," he said and turned around.

Caleb scrambled after the lurking shadow as the man walked to the looming farmhouse. The man went in through the side door and Caleb followed him into a washroom.

"Take off your shoes," the man said.

Caleb fumbled with his shoestrings. His fingers were so stiff, they didn't want to function, but he finally managed to get his shoes off. The man lit a lantern and then Caleb could see his face clearly. The tall, heavy-set man looked familiar with his brown hair and beard streaked with gray.

"Hold on, there," the man said, peering more closely at Caleb. "Ain't you the Swarey boy?"

Caleb gulped. He could deny it, but the man obviously recognized him. Now, the man would tell his parents and this whole running away business would be over. Caleb was humiliated to realize that his eyes were filling with tears. He blinked hard, trying to force them back, but it didn't work, they trickled down his cold, hard cheeks anyway.

The man cleared his throat. "I see. Well, get on into the kitchen. The missus will fix you something to eat, and then I'm taking you home."

"B-but—"

"Listen to me, son. Your folks are probably going out of their minds with worry right now. And after what they've been through, I don't think running away was a very *gut* move on your part."

"B-but—"

"They will be worried sick. How did you get here, anyway? Our farm is a *gut* ways out of town."

"I-I rode my bicycle."

The man raised his chin. "Did you now? Well, I'll be. You must have been froze solid when you landed in my barn. It's a wonder you're still breathin'. Get on into the kitchen, boy, before something worse happens."

Caleb had no choice but to obey. He shuffled into the kitchen where a plump woman was bustling about. She stopped short when she saw him. "Land's sake, child, where did you come from?"

"He was hiding in the barn," said the man who had followed him into the kitchen. "Can you fix him some breakfast, and then I'll be taking him home."

The woman gave her husband an inquisitive look but didn't question him. She finished flipping the eggs and took two fat slices of bread from the cutting board.

"Sit yourself down," she told Caleb.

He sat. The food smelled delicious, and he realized that he was next to starving. She gave him a glass of milk which he promptly guzzled. Then she set a full plate before him. She and her husband both watched him tuck into the food. He felt stupid with them gawking at him, but he shoveled in the food, nevertheless. Eggs and toast and bacon had never tasted so good.

The woman set about cracking more eggs into the cast iron skillet. The man sat down across from him. His cheeks were ruddy from cold and exposure over the years.

"So why don't you tell me and the missus why you took it into your head to run away."

Caleb swallowed a mouthful of food. He looked into the man's eyes and saw only kindness there. No judgement. No censure. Caleb's eyes brimmed with tears all over again.

"Now, Harold, you don't need to be bothering the boy before he's done eating," the woman said, giving Caleb a big smile. "Do you want more eggs?"

Caleb shook his head and licked his chapped lips. "*Nee*. I-I... This is fine."

"Well?" Harold said. "I assume you didn't get kicked out of the house."

Caleb shook his head again. "*Nee*."

"It's the guilt, *ain't so?* It's eatin' at you."

"Harold!" his wife cried.

"No sense dodging it, Mary Louise. The child is troubled."

Mary Louise set her lips into a disapproving frown.

"That shooting was an accident from what we heard." The man's voice gentled. Mary Louise sucked in her breath as she realized just who Caleb was. The man went on. "Ain't nobody blaming you, son. If that's what you're worried about."

Caleb was blinking rapidly. "B-but, it was my fault. My s-sister is dead because of me."

Harold sighed heavily. "*Jah*, that's true."

"Harold!" cried Mary Louise once again.

"Ain't any need to paint it another way. *Jah*, son, it was because of you. But the fact is—it was still an accident."

Caleb's stomach hurt. He shouldn't have eaten anything. The eggs and bacon were settling like bricks.

"Don't you think *Gott* has forgiven you?" Harold continued, almost whispering now.

Caleb looked into his eyes again and slowly, ever so slowly, shook his head.

Harold reached across the table and grasped his arm. "You're wrong. You're dead wrong. You can't see you're wrong because you're hurting."

"*Nee*," Caleb said, a sob nearly grabbing his voice away. "I ain't wrong. How... How could *Gott* forgive me?"

"Because He loves you, boy. And He knows you never meant it."

"I didn't," Caleb choked out. "I didn't mean it."

Mary Louise came rushing over. She put her arms around Caleb. "Of course, you never meant it. No one ever means it when they have an accident. You loved your sister."

"I-I did."

Mary Louise picked up a cloth napkin and dabbed at Caleb's

tears. “Hush now. Stop your crying. You’re going to be all right. You’ll see.”

Caleb shook his head. How? How in the world would he ever be all right again? And his mother and father and Levi? No one would ever be all right again.

Mary Louise dropped down onto the bench beside Caleb.

“Tell him,” Harold said. “Tell the boy.”

Caleb’s brow creased. What was he talking about? Tell him what?

Mary Louise rubbed her hands over her apron. “All right. All right.” She took in a big breath. “We had a daughter. Name of Jennifer, but we called her Jenny.” Mary Louise smiled, and Caleb saw a faraway look in her eyes. She was seeing something he couldn’t see. “*Ach*, but she was a pretty little thing. And happy. She was always smiling and making everyone around her smile, too. She had blonde curls.” Mary Louise laughed. “Never would stay proper-like beneath her head covering. We used to laugh together about that near every morning. Every year, she got sweeter. There was just something about her, you know? I don’t want to be vain, but she was the prettiest, nicest little girl in the whole world, she was.”

Caleb watched Mary Louise’s face. It was lit up, almost as if the lantern were shining directly on her.

“We loved her. We never had any more *kinner*. We don’t know why. *Gott* just didn't bless us that way. But we had little Jenny. Our Jenny." Mary Louise looked at Harold, whose eyes had misted over.

And even before Mary Louise went on with her story, Caleb knew. Jenny was gone. Jenny was in heaven along with Jodie. Inwardly, he winced. He didn't want to hear this story. He wished Mary Louise would be quiet.

"But then, our Jenny got sick. It wasn't nothing out of the ordinary. Flu, or so I thought. I wasn't too worried. I tended her. She seemed to be making improvements, until that one night."

She blinked and went on. "She got a fever. It was awful hot. Hotter than anything I'd ever felt. I put her in the bath. I put wet rags on her forehead, but it never helped. Harold went for Old Mae. But..." Another deep breath. "It was too late. By the time Old Mae got here, there was no help for it. Jenny died in my arms."

Caleb was crying now. He didn't know Jenny, never knew her, but he was crying for her.

"Don't you see? It was my fault. I should have called Old Mae sooner. I should have taken her to an *Englisch* doctor, but I didn't."

Harold wiped his eyes. "It was my fault too, wife. I never did those things either."

"The guilt ate at me," Mary Louise went on. "For years. Year after year after year, until one day... One day, I was done. I couldn't live like that anymore. My guilt never helped anything. It didn't bring my Jenny back. It didn't make me a better person. It was destroying my life and Harold's life. And then, I realized *Gott* had forgiven me long before. It was a knowing—deep in my heart. It was me who had held onto it. Not *Gott*."

She stared deeply into Caleb's eyes. "And who was I?" she asked, "Who was I to not forgive someone *Gott* had already forgiven? Who was I to place myself above *Gott*?"

Her gaze bore into Caleb. He squirmed, wanting to look away, but he wasn't able to. His throat was tight, and he was having trouble swallowing.

"But..." he whispered, wanting to protest. For her story was different. He had *shot* his sister. He had killed her outright. Not like Jenny. Jodie never was sick. Jodie was perfect until he — until he— He bit his lip and tried to stop the sobs, but he couldn't do it. He fell into Mary Louise's arms and cried. How was it possible that he had any tears left?

He cried for Jodie. And for Jenny. And for Mary Louise and Harold. And for his mother and father and Levi. And for himself.

Most of all, he cried for himself.

And Mary Louise let him. She snuggled him close and patted his back over and over and over.

"There, there," she murmured. "Let it out. That's right. Let it out."

He cried until there was nothing left to cry. He was suddenly so weak, he could hardly hold himself upright in a sitting position.

Mary Louise looked at Harold. "I'm putting him to bed. You go tell his folks where he is, but I'm putting him to bed."

Caleb was hardly aware of Mary Louise half lifting him from the bench, leading him upstairs and tucking him into a bed. But he felt the weight of the quilts on top of him, felt the soft pillow beneath his head. And then, just before dropping off into a deep sleep, he felt Mary Louise's lips gently kiss his cheek.

Chapter Eighteen

Levi was waiting for the first light to get underway. He was dressed, the animals had been seen to by lantern light, and he was waiting for his father. Odd that his dad wasn't up yet; usually, he beat Levi up and was almost done with the chores before Levi even got out there. But maybe, he was still sleeping. Levi wasn't sure when his father had fallen asleep. All he knew was that he'd heard sounds from his parents' bedroom until the wee hours—mumbling and crying.

Levi hoped his dad was sleeping, except the sun was about to come up and Levi wanted to get on the road immediately. He'd prayed that Caleb would show up during the night, but no such luck. Dear Lord, he hoped his brother was all right.

He went into the kitchen to start the tea. He could put a tray of sliced bread into the oven, too, and make toast. He tried to be quiet as he moved about the kitchen. Slowly, light filtered in through the window. By then, the tea was ready, and he was sipping a cup. The mug felt warm in his hands and he inhaled the steam.

He was buttering the toast when he heard something out front. He hurried to the window and saw a buggy approaching. He dropped the butter knife and rushed out the front door. Harold—Levi had forgotten his last name—climbed out.

"Harold?" he said.

Harold came around his horse and walked up to the steps. "Morning, son."

"Come in," Levi said. "What can I do for you?' His mind was whirling. Had his father made arrangements with Harold for something? Had Levi forgotten something?

"I'll make this quick," Harold said.

"My *dat*... Uh, shall I get him?"

"*Nee*. I can tell you just as easy. Your brother is with us," he said.

Before he could even continue, Levi's knees went weak. He leaned against the porch railing.

Harold tugged on his long beard. "He was hiding out in our barn. Spent the night there, I reckon. The wife has fed him and put him to bed. I would've brought him straight away, but she insisted he be put to bed. You're free to come by and pick him up anytime."

"He ... he was in your barn?"

"Discovered him early this morning." Harold shook his head. "A sad business, all right. I'm sorry for your family's loss. Caleb, your brother... Well, he's still upset about it."

"I know. I know he is."

"He'll be all right. Just give him some time."

Levi swallowed. "Thank you. Thank you for taking care of him."

"It's what we do," Harold said. "I'll be leaving you and gettin' back home now."

"Can I get you some tea?"

"*Nee.* I just wanted you to know so you wouldn't be fretting anymore." Harold shook his head. "A sad business," he repeated. "Real sad."

"Thank you, again," Levi told him and saw him out. And then he shut the door and raced up the stairs. "*Mamm? Dat?* You awake?"

He stuck his head into their room. It was still awful dark in there, but he could see both his parents stir at his voice.

"Huh?" his dad said, sitting up. "*Ach*, what time is it?"

"Harold's come by," Levi said quickly.

"Harold?"

"You know, Harold. I forget his last name. He's got Caleb."

"What?" his mother cried, stumbling out of bed. "What do you mean?"

"Caleb was hiding out in his barn. Harold found him. They fed him and he's in bed over there."

"What?" His mother seemed to be having trouble getting her mind around his words.

"Harold Mueller?" his dad asked, already taking his shirt from its peg on the wall.

"*Jah,* that's it. Harold Mueller."

"So he came by to tell us?" his mother asked.

"*Jah.* Caleb's all right, *Mamm*. He's fine. He's sleeping."

His mother sank back down to the edge of the bed. "Thank *Gott*," she whispered. "Thank *Gott*."

"We'll go fetch him," Walter said. "Levi, you ready?"

"I'm ready, *Dat*."

"Wait," his mother said. "Drink some tea first. It'll only take a minute. And I'm going with you."

"No need for you to freeze out there. Levi and I will bring the boy home."

Leah stood and faced her husband. "I'm going. He's my boy, too. I'm going to bring him home."

Walter shrugged. "Suit yourself, then. Hurry. And we don't need to be drinking tea before we go."

"It's already made," Levi told him. "I'll run down and pour you both a cup."

He left their room and ran down the stairs. His spirits soared. Caleb was all right. He was *all right.* In just an hour or so, he would be back home where he belonged. Gratitude welled in Levi's heart, and he found himself wanting to sing. Or hum. Or *something.*

He chuckled lightly. Such good, *good* news. He couldn't wait to tell Annie. She'd be so happy for them. But wait, she didn't even know Caleb was missing, did she? But Jason's family knew, and often news spread quick-like in Hollybrook. Well, if she did know, she was going to be mighty pleased that Caleb had been found.

He poured two cups of tea. Maybe he was being delusional. Likely Annie wouldn't care more than anyone else would. Goodness, but he was probably making something out of nothing. But he liked Annie. He really liked her. Maybe now that Caleb was back home safely, Levi could afford to think about Annie more seriously. Would she be amenable to him wanting to court her?

He heard his father coming down the stairs, and his mother right after him.

"You ready?"

"*Jah, Dat*. Come get your tea. I'll run out and hitch up Clipper."

Before his parents came into the kitchen, he was already out the side door and heading for the barn.

Annie opened her eyes and saw the morning light filter through the window. It was still weak, so it couldn't be very late. Still, she needed to get up. She'd spent the night in the big house instead of going back to the daadi haus the night before. In truth, she wasn't even sure why, but for some reason, she had wanted to be close to everyone. Maybe it was because she was leaving that day.

She tossed the quilts back and immediately shivered. Best get dressed right quick. She jumped out of bed and did just that, running to the bathroom when she was finished. She took a moment to use the toilet and splash water on her face.

The upstairs was still, so the children must all still be asleep. She figured that her uncle was already outside with the animals, but she didn't hear anything from the kitchen below. Maybe Thelma was getting a few extra winks of sleep.

Annie went back to the room and pulled back the curtains, letting in a bit more light. She had done her packing the night before. She wasn't going to be able to avoid her trip home. In truth, she would be happy to see her family, but she wasn't at all pleased about being forced to attend Matthew's wedding. Maybe, she could still get out of it. She could feign a headache or something. But the thought was distasteful. She didn't like to think of herself as weak. She raised her chin and took a deep breath.

She'd go to the wedding, and she would be cheery as if she'd never been to such a beautiful service. That was what she was going to do.

Her thoughts only dwelled on Matthew for a moment before they flipped over to Levi. How were the Swareys doing that morning? She imagined Levi was already up. Maybe Caleb was up, too, and the two of them were out in the barn working together. She hoped so. Levi had a wonderful way with his brother, and together, maybe they could help each other heal.

The night before, it hadn't taken her long to pack. She only needed to take enough things for a couple days. She wondered what dress she should wear to the wedding. Perhaps it was vain, but she wanted to look good. Maybe, she would wear her deep blue gown. That was her newest, and the blue brought out the color of her eyes—or so she'd always fancied. Yes. The blue one.

She let out her breath. She'd packed two gowns, including her blue one. She would likely have to iron it before she wore it to the wedding the next day. No matter how carefully she'd packed it, she knew it would be wrinkled when she got home.

She heard Thelma stirring then. She went to the door and peered out into the hallway.

"Morning, Annie," Thelma said, catching sight of her and yawning.

"Morning, Thelma."

"I hope you slept well in that bed. It was a bit lumpy last time I checked. But then, you didn't complain the first time you slept on it a while back, so I s'pose it was passable. I'll be getting breakfast together soon. I think I overslept."

"The bed was fine. I'll go down and start things..."

"Thank you. Give me a minute or two." Thelma disappeared into the bathroom.

Annie heard Bobby stirring. When he let out a wail, she went into his bedroom and scooped him up. "Shh, Bobby. We don't want to wake the others. Shall we go downstairs and fix breakfast? *Ach,* but first, I'll be changing your diaper."

She smiled and snuggled Bobby close, despite the odor from his bottom. She got him changed quickly, and they headed down the stairs. In the kitchen, Annie put Bobby on the floor and lit the lanterns.

"There. Are you hungry? How about some pancakes this morning? It won't take me long. And I'll give you the spoons so you can put them on the table. How about that?"

Bobby got up and toddled over to the utensil drawer and waited. Annie grabbed the spoons and handed them to him.

"There you go, pumpkin."

Bobby gave her a toothy grin and went into the dining area. Annie got underway with the pancake batter. She was just whipping it up when Henry came in.

"I'll be heading to the Swareys later," he told her.

Annie sucked in her breath. "What is it? What's happened?"

"Zeb, our neighbor to the north, just came by. He says Caleb's missing."

Annie's heart lurched. "What?"

"*Jah.* Caleb is *gut* friends with Jason, and his *dat* told Zeb that Walter and Levi were by last night. Caleb has gone missing. As soon as I eat, I'll be heading over there to help look. It ain't quite light yet, but after breakfast, it'll be plenty light to go looking."

"I'll help. I want to help, *Onkel*."

He tugged on his beard. "You need to be getting to the bus this morning. I don't rightly know—"

"I don't care if I miss the bus," she said hurriedly. "I want to help."

"You can't be missing your bus, Annie. Your *mamm* and *dat* would have my hide." He took off his hat and ran his hand through his hair, setting his hat on the counter. "You can come with me early. You can help look and then I'll drop you at the bus station. Will that suit?"

"Thank you," Annie said. She drew in a slow breath. What had Caleb done? Had he run away? What other explanation could there possibly be?

Thelma joined them in the kitchen. She took one look at her husband's face and said, "What is it? What's happened?"

"Caleb Swarey has gone missing. I'm going to help look for him after breakfast. Annie is coming with me. I'll drop her at the station in plenty of time."

Thelma's lips parted, and she shook her head over and over. "*Ach,* poor Leah. First little Jodie, and now Caleb is missing?" She looked at Annie. "You're going to help?"

"I want to."

Thelma nodded. "*Gut.* The more people looking, the better. I'd go, but what with the *kinner*, I wouldn't be much help. Maybe I could go over and sit with Leah..."

"Let's get eating," Henry said. He looked at Thelma. "I'll check in with you after I take Annie to the station. If need be, I'll take you and the *kinner* over to stay with Leah."

"Thank you," Thelma said. Her face had clouded over. "How much does the *gut* Lord put on a person?" she muttered, but Annie heard her and wondered the same thing.

Chapter Nineteen

Levi drove his parents to the Muellers' place. His father sat next to him, completely still and not talking. His mother sat behind him, and he heard her sniffing now and again. He wondered at that. Caleb was found—there was no need for tears anymore.

When he pulled up to the front porch of the farmhouse, Harold Mueller was quick to open the front door. He stood on the porch and beckoned them inside.

"He's still asleep," he said. "Mary Louise refused to wake him until you got here."

Leah pushed by Levi and hurried inside. Levi and his dad followed Harold.

"Ah, you're here," Mary Louise said, approaching them from

the kitchen. She took Leah's hands in hers. "Bless your heart," she murmured. "He's upstairs, asleep. Come with me."

The two women went upstairs. Levi was too eager to wait patiently downstairs. He followed them up, quietly, keeping his distance. His mother and Mary Louise disappeared into a room. He went to the doorway and stood, peering inside. His breath caught when he saw his brother sleeping peacefully on the bed. *Ach*, it was good to see him, and he looked none the worse for wear.

"Son," Leah said gently, sitting on the edge of the bed. "Son, it's me. *Mamm*."

Caleb stirred. Mary Louise smiled at no one in particular and tiptoed from the room, squeezing Levi's arm as she left.

Caleb stirred but didn't open his eyes.

"Caleb," Leah said. "Wake up, son. It's time to go home."

Levi went into the room and stood by the bed. "Caleb, wake up."

Caleb stirred again, and his eyes fluttered open. He gave them a look of confusion and rubbed his eyes. And then Levi saw the clarity come.

"*Mamm?*"

"We were worried." His mother's voice caught. Levi could tell she was ready to cry, but she held back.

"You weren't supposed to find me," Caleb said, wriggling to a sitting position.

"What? Why not?" Levi couldn't help but ask.

Caleb's gaze flickered to Levi and then back to his mother. "I know y-you don't want me no more."

"What?" Leah cried.

"After what I done, I don't blame you." Caleb's voice was choked with pain.

"That ain't true," came his father's voice from the doorway.

Levi turned to see Walter stride into the room. He hadn't even heard him come up the steps.

"That ain't true," Walter repeated. He went to stand beside his wife. "We need you at home, son. And we don't want any more of this running away."

"Where were you going?" Leah asked. "And you slept in a barn? In this cold? *Ach*, Caleb, what were you thinking?"

Levi knew Caleb hadn't been thinking at all. Not really. He'd just wanted to get away. To escape. Levi knew the feeling well.

"I think there's something both you boys better get through your heads." Walter's glance took in Levi, too. "Jodie's death was an accident. Plain and simple. A terrible accident. Your *mamm* and I... Your *mamm* and I don't hold blame for either of you. And neither does *Gott*. I don't want any more of this foolishness. It's bad enough to have lost our little girl. It's enough."

His expression turned firm, and Levi knew his father would tolerate no more.

"Do you both hear me? Your *mamm* has gone through enough. We need to draw together, not apart."

Caleb gulped and tears spilled from his eyes. "But I don't see how *Gott* will forgive me."

Walter grabbed his hand. "He already has, son. It's done. Over."

Leah wept with Caleb, and Levi felt a rock of tears shift in his throat. Maybe he hadn't run away like Caleb had, but he felt the same. Felt the guilt. The shame. The responsibility. Here Levi had been praying for his brother to heal, to feel better, to let go of his guilt, when he was mired just as deeply in it. He swallowed hard. His father claimed that forgiveness had already happened. That it was over.

Was it? Could Levi possibly believe it for himself—and not just for Caleb.

His father was staring at him now, and Levi blanched.

"You too, son," Walter said. "You heard me."

Tears burned the back of his eyes. He watched Caleb collapse in his mother's arms. Watched them hold each other. Cry together. Caleb's sobs were different this time. They were cleansing sobs. Levi had no idea how he could tell the difference, but he could. Maybe it was the look on Caleb's tear-stained face. Maybe it was the way he clung to their mother.

"Son?" Walter said, his eyes still piercing Levi.

And slowly, Levi nodded. It wasn't over, not by a long shot. But maybe, just maybe, he could accept that it was beginning to be over. That he could heal. That maybe, he was forgiven and that someday, he would think of Jodie again without cringing with pain and guilt.

He nodded again to his father, this time meaning it. He felt something stir inside. Not much, only the slightest whisper of a feeling. But that whisper was hope. He recognized it and latched onto it with his whole heart.

Jodie would want them to be happy. She was such a happy girl herself. She'd never want them to suffer. Never.

"Come on, son," Walter said. "Let's go home."

Leah stood up and helped Caleb out of bed. Then Walter drew them all in for a hug. It was so uncharacteristic of him, so tender and emotional, that Levi was stunned. But it felt good. It felt good to be enclosed within everyone's arms. Caleb gulped loudly and made a funny noise in his throat.

"You huggin' us all, *Dat*?" he finally got out.

Walter gave a low, thick chuckle. "It won't happen again," he said, letting go with a big grin.

Levi smiled in spite of himself. Then he grabbed Caleb to his chest and hugged him hard. "All right," he said to his brother. "You heard *Dat*, let's go home."

Annie gave Thelma a huge smile. "I'll be back before you know it," she said.

"We'll miss you, Annie." Thelma's look turned pensive. "You are coming back, *ain't so?*"

Annie nodded. "Of course, I am. I'm growing attached to Hollybrook." She laughed. "Well, in truth, I'm growing attached to you and the *kinner* and *onkel* and the folks here in Hollybrook."

Especially Levi, her mind rang out.

"I'm glad to hear that," Thelma said. "I've become accustomed to you being here, and I like it."

Annie smiled again. "*Gut*-bye, *Aenti*." She hurried out of the house, thinking now about the Swareys. They must be beside themselves with worry. She climbed into the buggy and Henry snapped the reins.

"Do you know any more about Caleb?" Annie asked.

"Just what I told you," he replied. "You can help me search for about an hour or so before I take you to the bus. We'll check first with the Swareys and see where they've looked so far."

"All right." Annie chewed her bottom lip. "Do you think we'll find him?"

"Of course, we'll find him," he said, nodding. "Caleb couldn't have gotten far. He'll be all right. You'll see, Annie."

Annie prayed with all her heart that her uncle was right. She leaned forward slightly in her seat, willing the buggy to go faster. Willing it to get to the Swareys quickly so they could help. When Henry finally pulled into the Swareys' drive, she was practically out the door before he even stopped.

"*Nee.* You sit tight," Henry told her. "I'll go check."

Annie let out her breath in a gush and prepared to wait, but Henry barely got out of the buggy before Levi appeared at the door. He met Henry halfway. Annie couldn't stay in the buggy any longer. She jumped out and rushed around to the bottom of the porch steps.

Her uncle was nodding his head. "I'll go inside and talk to your *dat*," he said and disappeared inside.

Annie looked up at Levi who was smiling at her.

"What is it? Did you find him?"

Levi nodded. "We did, Annie. He was hiding in the Muellers'

barn, and Harold Mueller found him. He's inside now with *Mamm* and *Dat*."

Annie was so overjoyed that she felt weak. "I'm so awful glad," she said, her voice a bit breathless. "I was worried."

Levi stepped down to meet her at the bottom of the stairs. "Were you?"

"I was."

His eyes on hers were so tender that she sucked in her breath. "I knew you would be worried. I... Well, I was eager to let you know."

She swallowed and felt as if she were falling into his eyes. She blinked rapidly and knew she should take a step back, but she couldn't do it. Instead, she leaned forward until she could feel his breath on her face.

"I just heard. I couldn't imagine it if you didn't find him," she spoke in a near whisper. "You must have been frantic."

"I was. We were." He searched her eyes as if looking for something. She wasn't sure what he was seeking. All she knew was that her affection for him had grown over the last days. Grown so quickly and so strong that she was nearly overcome with it. Could he see it? Could he see it in her eyes?

And then she did back away, suddenly unsure. Wondering whether she was once again going to make a fool of herself.

"Annie?" he said and then hesitated.

"*Jah?*"

She could see the indecision on his face. The hesitancy. What was it? What was he going to say? But her uncle interrupted them by coming back out the door, and she realized she would never know.

"*Gut* news, Levi," Henry said, joining them and clapping Levi on the back. "Such *gut* news. He told you then, Annie?"

Annie nodded. "He told me."

"We'll be leaving you alone then. Annie is heading back to Linder Creek today. Did she tell you?" Henry asked.

Levi looked instantly bewildered, and then he stared at Annie as if wondering why she hadn't told him. "You're ... leaving?" he asked.

"I... *Jah*. I'm going home—"

Levi cut her off before she could explain her reason, saying, "You're moving back? Today?"

"*Nee*," she said. "I'm only going back for a few days."

His shoulders relaxed, and he looked flushed. "I see."

"I, well, I have to—"

He shook his head. "I'm sorry. There was no reason why you should have told me. Have a nice time visiting your family."

He nodded at her and waved at Henry, who had already

gotten into the buggy. Then without a word, he turned and went back inside. Annie stood for a second, feeling lost. Levi had gone back indoors so quickly, she felt suddenly bereft. What had just happened? Was he hurt that she hadn't told him she was leaving? But that couldn't be right.

Goodness, but she sometimes twisted things in her mind. She gave herself a good shake and got into the buggy.

"You ready?" Henry asked her.

"I'm ready," she said.

Chapter Twenty

It felt downright strange to be back in Linder Creek. Annie hadn't been gone that long, but it felt like it. She'd changed—she could feel it way down to her toes. She wasn't the same girl who had left her home devastated such a short time before. Now, she was glad to see her family, but she didn't belong there anymore. She didn't belong in Linder Creek.

She belonged back in Hollybrook where she was learning to work the computer. Where she was reunited with her friend, Marlene. Where she was constantly helping Thelma with the children. She had purpose there. New friends there.

And Levi was there.

She longed to be back in Hollybrook the minute she stepped off the bus in her hometown.

"You're home!" her sister Betty cried, rushing to give her an embrace. "I came with *Dat* to get you." She made this announcement as though it weren't completely obvious.

"I'm glad to see you," Annie said, tugging lightly on her sister's *kapp* strings.

"*Mamm* made cinnamon rolls for you," Betty announced, "since they're your favorite."

"That they are," Annie said, collecting her suitcase from the luggage compartment.

Her father stepped forward. "It's *gut* you're home, daughter. I was quite sure you'd be on the bus today. Your *mamm* was worried you hadn't gotten her letter since you didn't write back."

"I only just got it. There wasn't time to respond."

Annie wanted to ask him right then why he'd insisted on her presence at the wedding. There seemed to be no reason for it, no matter how many times Annie pondered it, but she didn't want to ask him in front of Betty. In truth, she didn't know if she would ask him at all. She didn't think it wise to appear as if she were questioning her father's authority the minute she arrived home.

"Your brothers and your *mamm* will be right happy to see you." He took her suitcase from her and put it in the back of the buggy. "Get in, girls. It's still winter, you know. And cold."

Neither Annie nor Betty had to be told twice. They climbed right in and when their father joined them, they were off. Betty kept up a constant stream of chatter during the ride home. She was full of news of the upcoming wedding, and Annie wasn't required to say a thing about it, which suited her fine.

Betty leaned close to Annie. "Don't you think it's romantic that they got special permission?"

Annie forced a smile.

"Because they just couldn't wait. I hope someday I have a beau who can't wait to marry me..."

"Betty," came their father's voice, "enough of this foolish talk now."

"Sorry, *Dat*," Betty replied, not in the least discouraged. "But I'm not such a little girl anymore, you know. I know about things."

Annie's brow raised. Betty was indeed still a little girl. When in the world did she latch onto such a silly notion?

"I said that's enough now," Josiah reiterated, snapping the reins again. "Annie, how are our kin?"

"They're fine. Thelma told me to hurry back."

"I'm certain she did. So, you're a big help then?"

"I hope so." Annie bit her lip and then said, "*Dat,* I am going back, aren't I?"

He turned to look at her. "Why would you think otherwise?"

She opened her mouth but then closed it again.

"You're just here for the wedding, daughter. That's all."

She nodded. The wedding. The wedding. The wedding. How was she going to feel when she heard and watched Matthew vowing his love and loyalty to Doris?

"He ain't her cousin, you know," Betty said, glowing as if she carried the most delicious secret. "We all thought they was cousins, but they aren't. Not by blood. That's what *Mamm* told me. Not by blood."

"For goodness sakes, child," said Josiah. "I should have left you home."

Betty looked momentarily hurt, but then she smiled. "*Nee*, you wouldn't have. You knew how much I wanted to come get Annie." She grabbed Annie's hand. "I'm ever so glad you're home, Annie."

Annie's heart warmed. She had missed her little sister. True, she tended to talk too much at times, but she was a dear little thing.

"Annie's ears will be plumb worn off," Josiah said. "But here we are."

He turned the buggy into their drive, and Annie sucked in her breath. This was the first time she'd been away from home for so long, and it was lovely to see the tall white farmhouse again. It looked the same as it always did—somewhat stately, though well-worn. Two rockers sat on the porch, despite the cold weather. The wood stack to the side of the house was plentiful and covered by an old tarp. She saw the chickens fluttering about in the coop beside the barn. The flower beds lining the front of the house were barren now, colorless in the bleak winter landscape. The naked trees out front rustled slightly in the breeze, and she imagined hearing the branches creak and crack, the way they did when they were covered with ice. But they weren't covered that day, and there were only spotty patches of left-over snow dotting the yard.

"You girls go on in, I'll see to the horse."

"Thanks, *Dat*," Annie said.

"And I'll bring in your bag, so don't worry about that. Just go on in and see your *mamm*."

Annie's two younger brothers poked their heads out of the barn and waved at her. She waved back and then Betty tugged her across the yard to the side door. They were no sooner inside the washroom than Violet greeted them.

"*Ach*, Annie. You're home."

"Hello, *Mamm*."

Violet looked her up and down. "I guess your *aenti* is taking *gut* care of you."

Annie bit her tongue. She was far beyond needing an aunt to take care of her, but she responded, "*Jah, Mamm.*"

Violet clasped her in a quick hug and then led her into the kitchen. The aroma of fresh cinnamon rolls filled the air. Annie took a deep breath of their sweetness. Her mother wasted no time in handing her one on a napkin.

"Here you are, Annie."

"Thank you. It was right nice of you to make them."

"It ain't every day that a daughter comes home after being gone so long."

"*Jah*," said Betty. "It was way too long."

"Not really," Annie said, but she smiled and took a big bite. The roll tasted like home and love and all that was familiar. "So *gut, Mamm.*"

"Can I have one?" Betty asked.

"*Nee.* You'll spoil your dinner."

"But Annie got one!"

Violet raised a brow, and Betty clamped her mouth shut. "Betty, why don't you go on upstairs and make sure everything is in order in your sister's room?"

"It is. I already made sure."

"Betty," their mother said again, "why don't you go on upstairs and check?"

It was clear that Violet wanted to speak to her alone, Annie thought. She nudged her sister. "I'll be up in a minute with my suitcase, and you can help me unpack."

Betty seemed none too pleased, but she left the room.

Violet looked deeply into her eyes. "How are you, daughter?"

"I'm fine, *Mamm*. Truly."

"I wasn't the one insisting that you come home for this wedding," she said.

"So why is *Dat* wanting me here so badly?"

Violet took in a deep breath. "I don't know. He won't talk about it much, just kept telling me to write and make you come home."

"I'm not that excited about attending."

"Of course, you're not. But it will be over quick-like."

"When are any of our services ever quick-like?"

Violet burst into laughter. "You're right at that, daughter." She sobered and took Annie's hand. "But I'm glad you're home, whatever the reason."

"Me, too," Annie said and was surprised to realize that she

meant it. It was nice to be there in the warm kitchen with her mother. Nice to laugh together. Nice to smell the cinnamon and frosting of the fresh rolls.

"You better get on upstairs," Violet said. "Betty is beside herself with excitement. I'll bring up your suitcase."

"Thanks, *Mamm*," Annie said. She smiled at her mother and left the room to find her sister.

Chapter Twenty-One

Levi was sleepy. The scant sleep he'd gotten the night before was catching up to him. But now, Caleb was home and his mother and father were grateful. The house was quiet, unnaturally quiet as everyone went about their chores. Caleb had slept most of the morning away after their mother had forced him to eat another meal, even though Caleb claimed to be full.

Levi chuckled. His mother was happiest when she was feeding people. Cooking and baking and serving others were how she showed her love. Levi had seen it time and again over the years. He'd learned to eat nearly whatever she offered him now, just to make her happy. That morning, Caleb hadn't protested too hard against eating, likely realizing the same thing—whether consciously or unconsciously.

Levi felt more peaceful than he'd felt in weeks. Since Jodie died, to be sure. He wondered if this meant that things would be better now. That maybe, they were ready to begin the healing process, because in truth, they had all been raw with grief and guilt and who knew what else. His parents didn't talk about Jodie's death much. But he saw something on their faces this morning when they brought Caleb into the house. He saw something that had been missing from their expressions since the accident—a peace or maybe it was contentment. He wasn't sure which; all he knew was that they looked better somehow, more like their usual selves.

He prayed Caleb would be all right. Or at least that he would stop feeling such heavy guilt. Maybe running away had been the best thing for him—it seemed to have brought some things out in the open.

He went into the washroom and plucked his heavy coat from its peg, putting it on. He stepped outside and breathed in the cold air. He heard one of the goats bleating and grinned. Likely, it was Rascal. He'd no doubt gotten into something he couldn't get out of. Levi strode across the frozen ground and stepped inside the barn. He waited a moment for his eyes to adjust to the darkness inside and then he saw Rascal. He had fallen into a wheelbarrow that was full of loose straw and was snorting and fussing. Levi expected the critter to start sneezing at any moment.

"What are you doing, Rascal?" he said. "Well, get out if you don't like it in there."

But it was their deepest wheelbarrow and for some reason, Rascal's hooves kept sliding in the bits of straw, landing him on his side. Levi couldn't help but laugh. Just as he neared the wheelbarrow to help the poor thing, Rascal got a foothold and made a perfect flying leap onto the barn floor. He gave Levi a triumphant look tinged with a bit of disdain, tossed his head, and then proceeded to walk straight over to an empty grain sack that was hanging on a nail and chomp on it.

"Rascal, get back over here. I'm putting you into your pen. What else have you chewed up today?" But Levi didn't bother to look. He merely grabbed the goat's horns and tugged him into his pen, which was high enough to discourage any jumping out.

He fastened the latch and stood back, watching the goat rub his side up against the wooden slats of the pen.

"Stay put now, you hear?" he said. He looked around for something to do, some chore, something that needed fixing. He was restless all of a sudden, and he knew why. He wanted to go see Annie. But of course, by now, Annie was gone. She said she'd be back, but he wasn't completely confident of that. What if she got back to Linder Creek and wanted to stay? What if she never came back? What if he never got to see her again?

He gave a soft snort. How ridiculous. Linder Creek wasn't that far away; if he really wanted to see her, he could get on a bus and go. He wondered how she'd react to that. Well, there was no use getting the cart before the horse, was there? She said she'd be back, so she would.

"Do come back, Annie," he whispered into the air. "Come back so I can court you."

Because there was no doubt in his mind anymore. He was falling for her, and he wanted to get to know her. He wanted to know everything about her. What was her favorite color? Her favorite sweet? What did she like to do if she got a free minute? He longed to see her smile right then. She had a lovely smile. In truth, he hadn't seen it very often, but wasn't his family at fault for that? Things hadn't exactly been cheerful around Hollybrook these days.

But that was changing. Improving. He vowed right then that he was going to be the cause of her smiles when she returned. Goodness, but it would feel good to smile. And then he realized that he was already smiling just thinking about it.

Ach, Annie—you've crept straight into my heart.

There was no reason for the Hershbergers to be early to the wedding. None of them had a part to play in the ceremony. So Annie was surprised when her father announced that they'd be leaving the house at seven that morning. The service wouldn't begin until eight-thirty, and it certainly didn't take an hour and a half to get to the Glick farm.

For some reason, her father seemed bent on dragging this out for Annie. As she finished getting ready, she paused for a moment to assess exactly what she was feeling. Was she over Matthew? Her pulse quickened. Was she? Right then, she felt nervous, and her stomach was rumbling even though she'd eaten breakfast. If she was over Matthew, she wouldn't feel this way, would she?

Odd, but she wasn't missing Matthew. Not anymore—not really. In truth, the only reason she'd been thinking of him at all was because of this wedding and her father's insistence that she attend. Wasn't that a clear indication that she was over him?

But she couldn't put aside her nervousness. She brushed her hair until it was full of static electricity. It fairly cackled when she twisted it in a tight bun at her neck. She placed her freshest *kapp* on her head and then picked up the small hand mirror from her dresser. She stared into her blue eyes, looking for any hint of a broken heart.

She saw none. But there was a longing there, a yearning. It was clear to her, and it sent shivers up her spine.

But her longing had nothing to do with Matthew Wanner and everything to do with Levi Swarey. Annie sucked in her breath and went to her bed and sank down on the blue and white quilt. She pressed her hands against her chest. She was in love with Levi Swarey. It was painfully clear. She smiled and only just kept herself from laughing out loud.

She was in love *with Levi Swarey.*

And then she bit her lip. Was something wrong with her that she'd fallen out of love with Matthew so quickly and into love with Levi so quickly? She stood up and huffed. Goodness, but was she trying to create problems for herself? Couldn't she just enjoy the knowledge?

She smiled again, thinking of Levi. He and his family must be so happy. Maybe Leah Swarey was cooking a special meal to celebrate Caleb being home. Maybe Caleb and Levi were putting a puzzle together in front of the warming stove.

Was Levi maybe thinking of her?

She let out her breath in a rush. *Ach,* but she hoped so. She truly, truly hoped so.

"Annie! Come on down! *Dat's* waiting for us in the buggy!" her mother called up the stairs.

Annie rushed from the room, now eager to get this day underway. The sooner it was over, the sooner she could go back to Hollybrook, which was where—she quickly realized—she belonged.

Chapter Twenty-Two

Doris Glick looked lovely in her deep blue wedding dress. And there was no denying that Matthew was a very handsome groom. Annie observed them from where she sat, squished against the back wall of the Glick's front room. The room wasn't anywhere near big enough to hold all the guests, but by coming early, the Hershbergers were in the main room, not crowded into the dining area or even spilling out onto the front porch where the cold air was rapidly dropping in temperature.

Doris caught Annie's eye before the service began, and Annie could see the curiosity there. She knew Doris was wondering how she was doing. Annie knew Doris felt guilty for breaking her and Matthew up, but she'd done it just the same. Annie couldn't blame her. Doris loved Matthew and she always had. And Matthew loved Doris—*not* Annie.

How it had stung. How it had burned through Annie's heart with pain and bitterness.

But it was gone now. Annie only felt... What was it? She only felt a sense of rightness as she sat inside the Glick house. Doris and Matthew belonged together, and so when Doris looked at her, Annie smiled. A real smile. Not forced. Not bitter. Not accusing.

Doris's brow raised and then she broke out into a beautiful smile of her own. And just like that, things were all right between them again. Annie relaxed, her back touching the wall behind her. She glanced over to the men's side of the gathering and saw her father watching her. He nodded slightly, as if giving his approval. Annie's brow creased. Why was her father looking at her like that? He hadn't yet broken eye contact, and he must have seen her slight frown, for he nodded again, this time a little bigger. The look of approval was still on his face.

Annie's breath caught. So that was it. That was why her father had insisted she attend the wedding. He wanted her to close the door on the whole thing. He wanted her to watch Matthew become someone else's so she wouldn't pine for him anymore. Her forehead smoothed, and she let out her breath. Her father wasn't one to talk about feelings. In fact, her father was not one to show affection, either. But right then, she felt his love stronger than she ever had. He was watching out for her. Her mother must have shared everything with him, and he knew she needed to come that day.

She wouldn't have come—not without his insistence. And she might have always wondered if she was over Matthew. She glanced again at her former beau as he sat beside Doris at the front of the room. She felt... only kindness toward them both.

She glanced back at her father. He still watched her. This time, it was she who nodded. She smiled, and her father smiled back. Evidently satisfied, he turned his attention from her and back to the bishop, who had now risen and taken his place at the front of the gathering.

Annie suppressed her smile then and she, too, focused on the bishop. But her mind wasn't on the service. Nor the preaching. Nor the promises given in public.

Her mind was fixed solidly on Levi Swarey and the community of kind, loving people back in Hollybrook.

After the wedding and amidst all the hubbub of the wedding dinner and games, Matthew approached Annie. She looked up at him in surprise.

"You came," he said simply.

"I came," she answered.

"Thank you." He searched her eyes, and deep in her heart, Annie knew what he was looking for.

"I'm happy for you, Matthew," she said softly.

He let out his breath. "Are you? Truly?"

She laughed gently. "I am. Truly."

"Thank you, Annie. Thank you. We can be friends, then?" He looked hopeful.

"*Jah*," she assured him. But they wouldn't be friends. Not really. For she wouldn't be around, and even if she were, it would be too strange. Still, she harbored no ill feelings.

He smiled at her, and she returned his smile. She felt a delicious freedom sink down deep within her. She still loved Matthew. She likely always would, but in a different way. A different kind of love. Her eyes misted over as she realized the beautiful thing God had done for her. She looked away quickly, not wanting Matthew to be confused if he saw tears in her eyes. But it was all right. He'd already turned around, and she saw him looking for Doris. Doris met his eyes and they moved toward one another as if drawn by magnets.

Annie stood. She didn't need to be here anymore. She was free. All she wanted to do was go home and repack her bag and get on the next bus. Of course, the bus only came once a day for Hollybrook, and it wouldn't come again until morning. Still, she could squeeze her way outside and let someone else into the main room.

Her father must have been watching her because no sooner had she gone outside, but he was there.

"Annie?"

She turned. "Hello, *Dat.*"

"You ready to go back home?"

She paused, knowing he meant back to their farm, but home to her now meant someplace entirely different.

"*Jah*," she whispered, answering both his intent and hers.

He nodded.

"But I don't want you and the rest of the family leaving on my account."

He shrugged. "It's all right, daughter. I'll take you home and then come back and enjoy myself a bit longer."

They walked out to the buggy in companionable silence. Then her father said, "Go ahead and get in. It's cold out here, and I've got to hitch up."

"*Dat?*"

"*Jah?*"

"Thank you." She gave him a look, and he blinked and then nodded. She was thanking him for making her come back, making her face Matthew and Doris and their wedding, and she could tell that he understood.

"You're welcome, daughter." His voice was gruff and thick, and she was almost sure she saw a tear in his eye.

Chapter Twenty-Three

Levi was out of sorts. It was ridiculous, really. Annie had only been gone two days, but he felt her absence as if it had been a year. He had no idea how this kind of affection was even possible. He'd only know her for weeks. How had she crawled so surely right into his heart and mind? It was a mystery to him, but there it was. He was jumpy and couldn't concentrate on much of anything. His parents were so consumed with Caleb's return, that he hoped they didn't notice his restlessness, but no such luck.

"What's gotten into you, boy?" his dad asked as they worked together in the barn. He heaved a pitchforkful of hay down from the loft. "Caleb's home. We're doing better now."

"I know," Levi said, busying himself with putting the hay into the stalls.

"Well, you're making both me and your *mamm* nervous with all your stewing. What's gotten into you?" he repeated.

"Nothing. Just winter blues, I guess."

"The *gut* Lord made winter right along with spring and summer. It ain't our place to be preferring one over the other."

Levi didn't answer. He wasn't about to explain to his father that he'd fallen for the girl from Linder Creek. He couldn't explain it anyway—whoever fell so hard and so fast for someone? It didn't seem fitting, somehow.

But it *was* fitting. Levi loved her plain and simple.

What if Annie didn't come back? He sighed. Hadn't he already gone through this in his mind? He'd go after her. He'd go to Linder Creek and fetch her. *Please, please, please Gott, let her want to come.*

"Why don't you go chop some wood?" his father hollered down at him. "That might do you some *gut*."

Levi smiled. It would, at that. "Thanks. I will," he said, tossing his own pitchfork to the ground.

The next morning, Annie gave everyone a big hug. Her mother clung to her for an extra minute, and Annie nearly faltered. She supposed she could stay another day or two. But when her mother let go, Annie realized that she didn't want to stay. She needed to get back to Hollybrook. There was her job waiting for her. There were Henry and Thelma and the children waiting for her. There was even her old friend Marlene waiting for her.

And hopefully... there was Levi waiting for her.

Her father drove her to the motel parking lot which served as the bus station for Hollybrook. They waited inside the buggy until the bus came squealing to an airy stop in front of them.

"Bye, *Dat*," Annie said, grabbing her bag from the back.

"I s'pose it's time. *Gut*-bye, daughter. You write us now."

"I will." Annie gave him a quick hug and a smile and climbed out. Right before she boarded the bus, she turned and gave him another wave. He waved back and then snapped the reins. She watched as he left the parking lot. Gazing after him, she felt a momentary emptiness. Somehow, she knew she was saying good-bye to him for a long time. She had a certainty that she would never again live in Linder Creek, and in truth, she had no idea when she would visit again.

It was odd to think about. By this time, she had thought she would be married to Matthew Wanner and happily settled into her new home in Linder Creek. She might have been excitedly waiting for the news that she was with child.

Instead, she had resettled in Hollybrook, where she didn't yet know many people. Matthew Wanner was out of her life forever, and except for these last few days, she hardly thought of him anymore.

But perhaps most surprising of all—she was happy with how things had turned out. She anticipated a wonderful life in Hollybrook. She prayed that her new life would include Levi Swarey. She climbed into the bus, moved down the aisle, and found her seat. She settled against the vinyl headrest and closed her eyes. Levi's smile filled her mind. And his eyes—his gentle eyes, and the look of tenderness on his face. Surely, it had been affection for her she'd seen in his expression. She prayed she wasn't wrong.

Dear, dear, Lord, let it be true.

She placed a hand lightly over her lips and smiled. *I'm coming back*, she thought. *Levi, can you hear me? I'm coming back.*

Four hours later, Annie was unpacked and again settled in her little *daadi haus*. Thelma and the children were thrilled she'd returned, and she'd had to peel both George and Bobby off her legs to go out to unpack. Funny how she felt more at home in the little empty *daadi haus* than she'd had in her own bedroom in Linder Creek. But now, she was eager to get back to the big house and help Thelma make preparations for supper.

"Thelma?" she called, entering through the side door.

"In here," Thelma called back from the kitchen.

Annie went through and saw Debbie helping Thelma peel potatoes. Annie was pleased that Debbie had seemed to long ago get rid of her resentment of Annie's presence there. Debbie had even taken to coming out to the *daadi haus* on occasion, bringing her crayons and coloring books. The two of them had passed happy hours coloring and chatting together. Debbie had even opened up, telling Annie all about her *grossmammi* and the fun things they used to do together.

"Did you have fun at the wedding?" Debbie asked her now.

Annie nodded. "It was nice to see my family again, for sure and for certain."

"And the wedding?" Debbie asked.

Thelma's gaze flew to Annie, and Annie could see her concern. "Annie just got back, Debbie. Don't be smothering her with questions."

"I only asked if she liked the wedding. Ain't weddings supposed to be liked?"

Annie laughed. "It's all right, Thelma. And *jah*, Debbie, weddings are supposed to be liked."

"Was the bride pretty?"

"She was." Annie grabbed a peeled potato and proceeded to chop it into chunks. "In truth, she was real pretty. It was a nice wedding."

Thelma studied her. "And you were fine with it?"

"I was. In fact, totally fine," Annie told her. A look of understanding passed between them, and Thelma smiled.

"*Gut*," she said. "Now, let's get moving. Henry will be back from the shop soon, and I want this potato soup hot and ready."

Annie turned back to the potato she was chopping, but she couldn't stop thinking about Levi. Did he know she was back? She could hardly go to his house and announce herself. Would he have passed by the toy shop that day? If so, Henry might have mentioned that he'd picked her up earlier at the bus station. But how likely was it that Levi would have passed by the shop that day?

And this Sunday wasn't a preaching Sunday, so there was no hope of seeing him at service. She glanced through the kitchen window. It looked ready to snow again, so a leisurely walk down the road would be questioned. Besides, walking down the road was no guarantee of seeing Levi either.

She sighed.

It might be more than a week before she could see him again.

"How are the Swareys?" she blurted out before she could stop herself.

Thelma raised a brow. "Better—since Caleb came back. And

as far as I know, he hasn't strayed again. Interesting thing, though, about Levi..."

Annie's heart jolted. "What? What about Levi?"

"He's been coming into the shop all regular like these last couple days. Henry was right puzzled about it as Levi never really has anything to say." Thelma gave her a pointed look. "Would you happen to know anything about it?"

Annie's cheeks went instantly hot. "*Nee*," she muttered quickly, now putting her attention on the fresh dough Thelma had made for rolls. Annie punched it down and began kneading it, her mind whirling.

"Such a fine man is Levi Swarey," Thelma went on. "*Jah*. A fine, single man..."

Annie bit her bottom lip and felt the heat in her face increase. Debbie stopped washing the knives and turned off the water. "Why you sayin' that, *Mamm*? We all know he ain't married yet."

"Just mentioning interesting facts. Annie here doesn't know the district folk like we do."

Annie couldn't help but grin. "I know what you're doing, *Aenti*."

Thelma clicked her tongue. "Just watching for reactions, and I'm thinking I saw a pretty *gut* one just now."

Annie shook her head, but there was no use denying it. Thelma had come to know her too well.

“Debbie, how would you like it if we had company this evening for supper?” Thelma asked her.

Debbie perked up. “Who? Who you going to invite?”

“I'm going to invite Levi Swarey over. If he ain't free this evening, I think tomorrow will suit just as well."

"But how you gonna invite him?"

"Truth be told, I was fixing to go over to see Leah Swarey soon anyway. If you'll watch the *kinner*, Annie, I think I'll take myself over there this very afternoon.”

“I can watch the *kinner*,” Annie said, her pulse racing with the thought of seeing Levi so soon.

God bless her aunt for being so accommodating.

“Can I go too?” Debbie asked. “I'm almost done with these dishes.”

Thelma considered it. “All right. Why not? Annie, you'll just have the younger three, then.”

Annie nodded. “We'll get along just fine.”

Chapter Twenty-Four

Levi heard a buggy on the drive and drew back the curtains. "*Mamm*, you expecting anyone?"

Leah walked into the room. "*Nee*. Who is it?"

He watched Thelma and her eldest climb out. His pulse quickened. Was Annie with them? He waited, but both Debbie and Thelma shut their doors. His spirits sagged. Wasn't Annie back yet? Hadn't she said she'd only be gone a few days? In his mind, a few days had passed.

His mother went to the door and greeted the guests, ushering them inside. "So nice of you to come by," she exclaimed.

Thelma's gaze went directly to Levi. "Hello, Levi," she said.

"*Gut* afternoon. You, too, Debbie."

"*Mamm* wants you to come to supper," Debbie announced. She puffed out her chest as if she'd broadcasted vital information.

"*Ach,* Debbie. I was getting to that," Thelma gently scolded.

"To ... supper?" Levi questioned. This was odd. Thelma had never asked him to share a meal before. Particularly by himself.

Thelma looked at Leah. "You're all welcome to come, too," she said, looking as if she made that decision right on the spot.

His mother must have noticed, too, because she politely declined. "Thank you, Thelma, but we'll be staying home. I think... Well, it would be best for Caleb, I believe, if we keep things more normal-like right now." She looked at Levi. "But it would be nice for you to go, Levi."

Levi wanted to ask if Annie was back. The words were burning on his tongue, but he didn't let them out. That would make his feelings much too obvious, and he wasn't eager to give things away just yet.

"Thank you, Thelma. I'd be right glad to come," he said.

Thelma looked pleased. "*Gut.* You can come over anytime, but we'll eat about five-thirty."

"Thank you."

Debbie grinned. "Is Caleb here? Didn't he have new kittens or something?"

The kittens Debbie referred to were almost grown cats by then, so Levi smiled. "They're almost grown up now. But Caleb is here. I'll call him down."

Levi went to the stairs and called for Caleb to come down. When he did, Debbie asked if he had a puzzle or something to do."

Caleb gave Levi a look which clearly indicated he had no interest in putting together a puzzle, but nevertheless, he led Debbie into the front room to find one.

Thelma had gone into the kitchen with his mother and Levi felt momentarily at loose ends. He didn't want to work a puzzle, nor did he want to join his mother and Thelma in the kitchen. Where was his father, anyway? He'd gone out to the barn right after the noon meal to sharpen some tools. Was he still out there sharpening? Levi went to grab his coat. Spending the next hour or two sharpening tools suddenly sounded downright appealing.

Later that day, Levi bid his mother and father farewell and went outside to hitch up Clipper. While it had been windy all afternoon, it was now still, and the cold air didn't seem nearly as uncomfortable without the wind whipping. He got into the buggy, still wondering why Thelma had invited him over. Was Annie there? He figured she must be home, what other possible reason could there be for his invitation?

With that in mind, he'd changed into his best shirt, put on his newer suspenders, and fussed with this felt hat, brushing it clean with the hand brush in the washroom. He'd glanced at himself in the small mirror over the bathroom sink and decided he looked passable. Truth be told, he hoped he looked more than passable. There was a distinct light of eagerness in his eyes.

Goodness, but he was going to feel the fool if Annie wasn't there.

Despite the brisk air, Clipper seemed glad for the outing. Levi knew the horse well and sensed her excitement. Or maybe she was picking up on Levi's mood. It didn't take long to arrive at Thelma's and Henry's place. He drove up to the barn and unhitched Clipper, hoping he would be staying long enough to merit the unhitching. He put Clipper in the pen beside the barn with Henry's two horses. Then he took a deep breath and strode toward the house.

He was climbing the steps, when the front door opened. Annie slipped outside, smiling her welcome. His heart rocked. She looked so beautiful standing there. Her blue eyes glittered, and her smile mirrored the sun on its brightest day.

"Annie," he said, his voice tight and heavy with emotion.

"Hello, Levi," she answered. Her cheeks were flushed, whether from the cold air or excitement, he had no idea. "I-I'm glad you're here," she went on, and he was so taken by her sweetness and her warmth, that he had to stop himself from stepping close and sweeping her into his arms.

"You came back?" he asked, somewhat stupidly, for wasn't she standing right there in front of him.

Her smile deepened. "Of course, I did."

His chest nearly hurt with the beauty of her. He swallowed. "I'm glad."

She blinked and then bit the corner of her lip as if suddenly growing shy and unsure of herself.

And then, he did step closer. He felt her eagerness, and again had to stop himself from taking her in his arms. Their gazes met, and his heart turned over in response.

"Annie?"

"*Jah?*" She was breathless, and the cold air circling them somehow grew warmer.

"Can I... Can I court you?" He sighed in relief as the words poured from his mouth. There. He'd said it. Now, it was no longer an unspoken wish that pulsed within him to the point of bursting. She knew now. Knew how he must feel.

She pressed her sweet lips together, and her eyelids fluttered. He thought he saw tears there, but they were instantly gone.

He froze inside. Wasn't she going to say yes? Wasn't she going to agree?

She swallowed, and he feared she was going to burst into tears. What was going on? Had he misjudged her so hugely?

"Annie...?"

She nodded and two tears fell from her eyes. She brushed them away with the back of her hand.

"*Jah,* Levi. I want you to."

His pulse pounded, and he was filled with a dizzying ache for her. His heart danced with excitement. He carefully took one of her hands in his. And then, he leaned down and brushed his lips against her cheek. He felt her shudder, and he quickly looked into her eyes. She met his gaze and a slow, beautiful smile crept over her face.

"Are you hungry, Levi?" she asked. "We almost have supper on the table."

He *was* hungry. He was hungry to know her and love her and spend every waking minute with her, but of course, that wasn't what she had meant at all.

"I am hungry," he said simply, privately smiling at the double meaning as he followed her into the house.

The End

Continue Reading...

Thank you for reading ***Annie's New Beginning!*** **Are you wondering what to read next?** Why not read ***The Cousin?*** **Here's a peek for you:**

Doris Glick gazed at her aunt's sour expression. "I'm sorry, *Aenti*," she murmured, even though she wasn't sorry at all.

Eliza Troyer sniffed, drawing herself to her full height. "I should well think you would be sorry," she said, her voice clipped. "I made a promise to your *mamm*." Her face crumpled for a quick moment and then hardened in exasperation. "I haven't done my duty to you or to my sister."

"It isn't your fault. You can't take the blame."

"You're under my roof, *ain't so?* You're in my care."

"I'm also nineteen years old and hardly a child." Doris took a step closer to her aunt. "You've been wonderful *gut* to me, and I'm right grateful."

"What is it, then?" Eliza asked. "What is it about that boy that won't allow you to give him up? He's in prison, Doris. *Prison.*" She visibly shuddered. "Imagine an Amish boy in prison. It doesn't bear thinking about."

"He's getting out soon. And don't we all make mistakes? Isn't forgiveness what we're all about?"

Eliza gripped Doris's arm. "Maybe so. But that don't mean you have to be writing to him. That don't mean you have to be sweet on him."

"We can't choose who we're sweet on, can we?" Doris tried her best to inject a playful note into her voice, hoping to cajole a smile out of her aunt. It wasn't to be.

"This ain't no laughing matter, child." Eliza ran her hands down her ample bosom and then twisted her fingers in a nervous gesture. "What am I going to say to Henrietta?"

"You don't have to say a thing," Doris said, working to curb her anger. She wasn't a little girl who had to be tattled on to her mother.

"I promised I'd care for you—"

"Which you have."

"I promised I'd get that Lehman boy out of your mind."

Doris sighed. "It isn't that easy."

"Clearly, it ain't," Eliza said with a moan. She squared her shoulders. "There will be no more letter-writing to him, do you hear me? None at all. I won't have you writing lovesick letters under my roof."

Doris pursed her lips. Now Eliza was acting more like herself—taking charge, no questions allowed, instant obedience expected.

Thank you for Reading

If you **love Amish Romance**, **Visit Here:**

https://amish.subscribemenow.com/

to find out about all **New Hollybrook Amish Romance Releases! We will let you know as soon as they become available!**

If you enjoyed ***Annie's New Beginning,*** would you kindly take a couple minutes to leave a positive review on Amazon? It only takes a moment, and positive reviews truly make a difference. I would be so grateful! Thank you!

Turn the page to discover more Amish Romances just for you!

More Amish Romance for You

We love clean, sweet, rich Amish Romances and have a lovely library of Brenda Maxfield titles just for you! (Remember that ALL of Brenda's Amish titles can be downloaded FREE with Kindle Unlimited!)

If you love bargains, you may want to start right here!

VISIT HERE to discover our complete list of box sets!

http://ticahousepublishing.com/bargains-amish-box-sets.html

VISIT HERE to find Brenda's single titles.

http://ticahousepublishing.com/amish.html

You're sure to find many favorites. Enjoy!

About the Author

I am blessed to live in part-time in Indiana, a state I share with many Amish communities, and part-time in Costa Rica. One of my favorite activities is exploring other cultures. My husband, Paul, and I have two grown children and five precious grandchildren. I love to hole up in our lake cabin and write. You'll also often find me walking the shores by the sea. Happy Reading !

https://ticahousepublishing.com/

Made in United States
Orlando, FL
05 August 2022

20576767R00124